Born in 1989, Carlos Manuel Álvarez is a journalist and author. In 2013 he was awarded the Calendario Prize for his collection of short stories *La tarde de los sucesos definitivos* and in 2015 he received the Ibero-American Journalism Prize, Nuevas Plumas, from the University of Guadalajara. In 2016 he co-founded the Cuban online magazine *El Estornudo*. He regularly contributes to the *New York Times*, Al Jazeera, *Internationale*, BBC World, *El Malpensante* and *Gatopardo*. In December 2016 he was selected among the best twenty Latin American writers born in the 1980s at the Guadalajara Book Fair in Mexico and in May 2017 he was included in the Bogota39 list of the best Latin American writers under 40. *The Fallen* is his debut novel. He is also the author of *The Tribe* (Fitzcarraldo Editions, 2022), a collection of reportage, and the novel *Falsa Guerra* (forthcoming with Fitzcarraldo Editions).

Frank Wynne has translated works by authors including Michel Houellebecq, Patrick Modiano, Virginie Despentes, Jean-Baptiste Del Amo, Javier Cercas and Almudena Grandes. His work has earned various awards, including the IMPAC Prize (2002, 2022), the Independent Foreign Fiction Prize (2005), the Scott Moncrieff Prize (2008, 2016) and the Premio Valle Inclán.

'A beautiful and painful novel that demonstrates the power of fiction to pursue the unutterable.'
— Alejandro Zambra, author of *Multiple Choice*

'A war foretold that never takes place. A death foretold that never takes place. And in the middle of this is the inevitable collapse of a family and a country. *The Fallen* is a subtle, intelligent and profoundly moving novel which sketches, in elegant and thoughtful prose, a rarely seen Cuban landscape.'
— Alia Trabucco Zerán, author of *The Remainder*

'Álvarez does a neat job in this very short but nutritious novel of establishing the personalities of his characters firmly enough that it comes as a real shock when he upends our expectations of how they might behave.'
— Jake Kerridge, the *Telegraph*

'In a dysfunctional environment, deception invades private family life. The lines between truths and lies are blurred. In a poetic telling, this short novel explores the human capacity to love and to hurt.'
— *Irish Times*

'The best in Latin American literature is here: with the precocious skill of someone who is a paragon of narrative resources and sensitivity, Carlos Manuel Álvarez vividly portrays the only identity that really matters: not national, but human. *The Fallen* is a museum of solitude and of the cracks separating our inner world from the one we live in and from those with whom we coexist.'
— Emiliano Monge, author of *Among the Lost*

'In *The Fallen* every voice has its own music of sadness, its own rhythms of isolation, its own lexicon of defeat. This novel is a subtle masterpiece.'
— Juan Cárdenas, *El País*

Fitzcarraldo Editions
8-12 Creekside
London, SE8 3DX
United Kingdom

Copyright © Carlos Manuel Álvarez, 2018
c/o Indent Literary Agency, www.indentagency.com
First published in 2018 as *Los caídos* by Sexto Piso, Mexico
Translation copyright © Frank Wynne, 2019

This first paperback edition published in Great Britain
by Fitzcarraldo Editions in 2022

The right of Carlos Manuel Álvarez to be identified as the
author of this work has been asserted in accordance with
Section 77 of the Copyright, Designs and Patents Act 1988.

ISBN 978-1-80427-010-3

Design by Ray O'Meara
Typeset in Fitzcarraldo
Printed and bound by CPI Group (UK) Ltd

fitzcarraldoeditions.com

The Fallen
Carlos Manuel Álvarez
tr. Frank Wynne

For Rafael Alcides (1933-2018)
eternal prince, bridegroom of the world

'Everyone has a home and that's where the troubles begin.'
— Philip Roth

I

The Son

I call my mother on the phone to see if she's had a fall
and she says no. We are silent for a moment. I know how
things are at this time of day. She'll be worried that she
still has to put the lid on the simmering *frijoles*, frustrated
that the trash can is full and no-one's taken the trouble to
empty it, sad because the old wooden window frames in
the bedroom will carry on rotting for all eternity.

I'm fine, *hijo*, honestly, she says. She doesn't feel ill, she
hasn't had a dizzy spell and she remembered to take her
pills on time. From the ceiling hangs the yellow light of an
incandescent bulb. The glare melts us, the soldiers, dis-
solves the broken concrete columns, the stone benches,
the rusty railings and the roof gutter, sending us eddying,
for a moment, into the gullet of night. I say goodbye, hang
up the phone, leave the sentry officer's post and walk
back to the dormitory dragging my feet, with my boots
unlaced. My shirt's untucked, the shoulder strap of my
zambrán belt digging into my neck.

They came looking for me at home a few months ago.
Military service is obligatory at eighteen, but there are
ways of getting out of it. In the *barrio* where I live, some
guys dodge it with the help of their families, who fake
medical certificates for them with I don't know what con-
genital disease, or bribe the admissions board. If I had a
father who was reasonable, I could have got out of this
shit too, but no-one in my house dares to talk about bribes
or circumventing the law. Armando told me he was proud
that I was doing my duty, just like he did back in the day. I
kept my mouth shut and gave him a contemptuous sneer.
Armando didn't even notice. My mother did.

I can't get that moment out of my head – in fact it seems
I don't want to. It's like a fly you shoo away that comes

back and lands again and again. I don't have much time to rest now before my sentry duty. The stupid notion that my mother might have had a fall has cost me thirty, maybe forty minutes, who knows. It's not just the time it takes to walk from the barracks to the sentry post. There's also the time between the moment when the thought first occurs to you and when you decide to act on it.

You want to go back to sleep but you know you won't be able to; the raveled threads of sleep are like reeds you're trying to cling to. Wakefulness is pulling at you, sweeping you downstream. Your eyes are still closed, the other soldiers are still sleeping, and you refuse to believe that you're already awake – for a moment you try to convince yourself that you're still asleep and simply dreaming that you're waking up. And yet, something beyond your control has rattled into life.

You open the wooden dormitory door as cautiously as possible so that the hinges do not creak. You have no desire to wake anyone, to have boots thrown at you, you've already had your share of fights. The dorm is a room of four or five square meters in which everyone is both friend and enemy to each other, and friend and enemy to himself.

At 10.30 p.m. insects are fluttering around the bare yellow bulb on the quad, a background hum that grows louder as the night wears on. Anything that breaks the silence clearly benefits the soldier and his mental health. You walk along the hall, your gaze sliding off things, seeing nothing in particular, as though the objects, forms and concepts that make up the world refuse to be observed. You come to the sentry post, reach through the double window behind the rusty iron railing and pick up the desk phone.

The officer of the watch is asleep, a big-hearted captain

who has come down in the world, like all the lieutenants or captains or lieutenant-colonels that make up this military unit, filled with alcoholics who wasted their lives hoping for and preparing for a war that never came, or that came in a different form, crawled inside them and gnawed away at them from the inside.

You dial the number of your house, recognize your mother's voice, decide to speak in a normal tone, and you mother answers normally. Then you fall silent for a moment and go back to your dormitory. Your shirt untucked, your boots unlaced, your *zambrán* belt digging into your neck. It is going to take you twice as long to get to sleep again. You don't know why your mother sometimes talks as if she were mentally retarded.

You tell yourself it's the disease, but what does that mean? You tolerate this woman who sometimes takes over the body of the mother you know and who you go on calling mother even when there is nothing left of her that bears the slightest resemblance to the mother you knew, except, maybe, certain physical traits, and not even that, because, from what they say, in the ugliness that follows the falls, your mother's lucid gaze is replaced by a vague, trancelike stare; her mouth, usually filled with comments and remarks becomes dry and twisted, the lips curl into a strange rictus; the skin, warm and pulsating like the skin of all mothers, becomes a pale, withered hide, and her lithe, hyperkinetic body becomes a slow, misshapen mass, flat, motionless, affording no shelter.

There is a little less than an hour before your watch. You hear the limping beat of your heart just below your ear, as though your heart were in the pillow, a toad hiding in the pillowcase. It is an uncomfortable throbbing, but it is the first sign that you are falling back to sleep: the ear turns and begins to listen inwardly. Then you notice something vague, like the pain in your joints becoming a pleasant ache.

You do not try to cling to anything, you simply let yourself be carried by the current, like a broken body, until you get caught in a clump of reeds, or some whirlpool sucks you under, or you wash up on some sandbank, and then your last thought is that now you are going to sleep and that this, the fact that you are going to sleep now, is the last thought that you will have for now, that afterwards there will be nothing left inside your head, and afterwards there is nothing.

The Mother

I'm alive and in my panties and my skin is yellow. I'm a heap lying on top of the bed, the dirty sheets. By the time I finally get up, my arms are covered in goosebumps. I open the wardrobe, put on a housecoat and go into the kitchen. Armando is making coffee. His movements are slow, graceless. The way he holds the coffee pot, the way he turns on the gas, the way he strikes the match and holds it to the ring. He is so slow that his every action already contains within it its own repetition.

He looks at me and smiles and there is something in his smile that unsettles me. He asks me if I want coffee. I say yes, a little. I ask him how he slept and he says better than most nights. I ask him if he had a dream and he says no. He says this as if I already know, but how could I know something I have no reason to know? I don't ask any more questions.

He hands me the coffee. The two of us go into the living room and sit in the mahogany rocking chairs. The back of one of them is broken. I turn on the TV, I like watching TV even when I'm not really watching or when there is nothing to watch. The handle of my coffee cup is broken. It's tiny, the sort of handle you have to hold by slipping one finger through it, and people with fat fingers have to hold on the outside, using their forefinger and thumb as a pincer.

Armando rocks gently, but the chair rattles. When he thinks I've finished, he asks for my cup so he can wash it. I tell him I'll do it. He goes into the dining room, fetches his shoes, his dark socks, his freshly ironed shirt and comes back into the living room. Like most men who pride themselves on being well informed, Armando watches TV in the morning while getting dressed. It's not yet seven o'clock. Already they've started broadcasting the same news stories they'll be broadcasting for the rest of the day, the same news they've been broadcasting my whole life. The truth is, I enjoy it.

I take the two cups to the sink in the kitchen. Armando goes to our daughter's bedroom to wake her. He hugs her. He always used to wake Diego more gruffly, though not without a certain tenderness. He'd jokingly bark military orders, calling Diego a miserable little runt, and drag him out of bed. I asked Diego and he said that's not how they wake you when you're doing military service, that he has no idea where his father came up with these orders.

I dry the counter, put the coffee pot in a corner behind the tub of washing-up liquid. I look at my kitchen, at my domain. I start tidying up, even though the neurologist has advised me not to. There's a secret force in the labors of a housewife. It doesn't stultify you, I don't care what people say. Arranging the plates in the draining rack according to size, storing the glasses upside down so they dry properly – I find these things calming.

My daughter says good morning and kisses my neck. Then she heads for the bathroom. Armando picks up his briefcase, his car keys and comes over to say goodbye. He lays his hands on my shoulders, squeezes them a little. He's a handsome man. He has gray hair, a thick mustache, a husky voice. His nose is a little too thick, but his eyes are a deep, translucent black. His complexion is brown, a smooth summery skin.

Armando tells me I suffered tonic-clonic seizures last night. I ask whether he managed to soothe me. He doesn't answer. He tells me to take it easy and urges me to hang up immediately if there are any more strange phone calls. I have no idea what expression is on my face, but Armando scoops me up and carries me back to bed.

María emerges from the bathroom, comes over and lays a hand on my forehead. I feel fine, I say after a moment. Armando sets off for work. I relax. María bustles in and out of the room, brings me my pills and a glass of water. I look at my pale, wrinkled feet, then look at myself in the mirror. My face is angular, barren.

There is a deep furrow that traces the edge of one nostril and runs into my lip, cleaving it. My lips like a piece of dried fruit, the thick breath from my mouth, my quivering neck, the scream stifled by my skin. My bovine eyes filled with damp resignation.

Deep within the mirror, standing motionless, a few meters behind me, the silent silhouette of my daughter. I go back into the kitchen, take the cup with the broken handle and put it in the bin. I take the coffee pot and pour the contents down the sink. I turn on the tap. Unfaltering, during this half hour, the TV news has continued to provide background music.

The Father

Days like rabid dogs. But I am an honest man and I endure, a man who knows that the heroes of our country endured much worse, a man who knows that real men hold their pain inside.

The car is out of gas again. A '95 Nissan, fairly new. I would have preferred a Lada, a Fiat, something cheap. That would have suited me. With a Lada, you can use spare parts from other models, it goes where you need it to go, and it would not have broken down on me the way the Nissan is doing. I am not complaining, I get by. It broke down for the umpteenth time and I left it there, halfway down the road, on the curb. I was sticking my hand out for half an hour before a bus picked me up. This has been happening a lot these past weeks, but I make do with the fuel I am allocated.

There must be a leak in the gas tank. At the maintenance department they said no, it's running perfectly. They could be pulling a fast one, I'm not ruling it out. Nobody likes their boss. I do not either, to tell the truth. But the difference is that my bosses are corrupt and I am an honest and irreproachable boss, like Che Guevara, who once visited a bicycle factory where the lickspittle manager tried to give him a bicycle for his daughter and Che put him in his place, saying that these bicycles weren't his, meaning the manager's, that they belonged to the State and he had no right to give them away.

These days people take what they are given, and sometimes what they're not given too. Sometimes I cannot help but think – not that I would say it, obviously – that the heroes of the Revolution had it easier than I do. People say times were hard back then, but the hardest times are those when no-one wants to

19

do anything, times marked by a crisis of values, a spiritual simple-mindedness, too little determination. The mechanics in the repair shop don't want to work. They spend their days sitting in the cars, smoking, telling stories or talking about everything and nothing, stuffed into their oil-stained overalls, pestering the women who walk down the street behind the hotel. The drivers and the grease monkeys and the auto body mechanics. They need a firm hand, the lot of them.

They look at me submissively, but you can feel the resentment oozing from every pore. You can see it when one of them heads out to tow my Nissan back to the hotel. It is not even nine o'clock and already they're hacked off. Sometimes this country is too kind to its people. It gives them so much in exchange for so little.

I go up to my office. On the way, a couple of workers greet me. My secretary tells me there is a pile of documents requiring my signature on the desk. She asks after Mariana, I tell her she is better, then she goes into the office kitchen to get me some coffee. My office is little more than spartan. A ceiling fan, a desk, a sofa, three chairs for meetings, a telephone, a desktop computer, photographs of my children, a glass pyramid paperweight, and a piece of wood in the form of a scroll carved with a quote from Ho Chi Minh. First to cross the river, last to arrive at the feast, it reads.

The secretary brings the coffee. I sip it slowly, it is a little bitter for my taste. I sign the pile of documents, all but one, sent to me by a Party official. I tell my secretary to arrange a meeting with him. For what time, she asks. One o'clock, I say, after lunch. My secretary is not young, she is not pretty, she is not discreet. She is an elderly woman in her sixties who has been working as secretary in hotels or in the tourism sector for two-thirds of her life, long before there was a tourist industry as such.

I make my daily round of the facilities: the laundry, the kitchens, the specialist restaurants, the beach bungalows. It is high season. By the swimming pool, I am forced to intervene when two Russians, having downed a bottle of vodka apiece, have come to blows and it is not even noon.

I eat lunch in the staff canteen. María comes over and asks if she can have a minute. She is the floor manager of the Cuban restaurant. María never beats around the bush. I like that about her. I realize we are living in an era where things are said with three times more resources, words and complications than necessary. It is almost impossible to work out what people are trying to say. María wants to talk to me about René. There is nothing to say, I tell her. She asks me to give him another chance. I tell her that I appreciate her work, that she is my daughter and I love and respect her, but could she please leave me in peace.

No-one else in the canteen talks to me. I arrive back at my office for the meeting with the Party official to find him sitting in the waiting room, reading the newspaper. I invite him in, open the door and usher him in ahead of me. The man despises me. A year ago, he ordered the hotel pastry chef to make a three-tier cake for his daughter's fifteenth birthday, and I canceled the order. I told him the story of Che Guevara and the bicycle. I am not entirely sure he got the point.

I tell him that I cannot sign the request he has submitted. He is asking me to authorize leave for a barman and a cashier so he can send them on military maneuvers for a whole month. Two of my best workers. He asks whether they are friends of mine; I say no. In that case, he says, I can send the barman and the cashier on military maneuvers and hire a barman and cashier from those already

21

approved as reserve staff. I ask why he does not send the reserve barman and cashier on maneuvers. He says fine, and leaves.

The afternoon drifts away, a Benadryl tablet the size of the sun. I feel drowsy, but I don't want to nap. I am reluctant to stir up the troubling images that, for some time now, have been coming to me in dreams. Insomnia is a clear symptom of wanting to be in control of one's life. My secretary asks permission to attend the parent-teacher meeting of her grandson, who has just started primary school, and I let her. After that, between making phone calls and reading the annual budgets, I get the day back on track.

Before going home at about six o'clock, I stand for a while next to the swimming pool, gripping my briefcase tightly. I feel the roiling chlorinated water, water flowing into water. I bend down, plunge my fingers in, press them against the return outlet, feel it suck. When I stand up again, I am already in the parking lot, in the Nissan, my briefcase on the passenger seat, and, without saying goodbye to anyone, I drive off.

Mariana has had another fall. María is already home. She leaves work before I do so she can catch the staff minibus. She picked her mother up from where she was lying on the living room floor, between one of the armchairs and the television, clutching the remote control. She has bumped her collarbone again, and split her chin. Right now, she is sleeping. I make dinner. I do not say as much, but I have no idea what what I am going to do, what we are going to do about this. María goes to her room.

I do my best. Beef stew, white rice and beans, a ripe avocado. I had to have a word with Mariana, I do not want her cooking or going anywhere near the stove. I do not want her using knives, I do not want her being consumed by the sweat exuded by the kitchen. But still she carries on, sneaking into the kitchen during the day, and then what happens, happens. My eyes are burning.

After a moment, I sense a shadow approaching. Almost reluctantly, she steps into the kitchen. She always wakes at around this time. She kisses the corner of my mouth. She is wearing a frayed housecoat. She is tall, her skin is very pale, her eyes are round but, despite everything, still luminous. All those bruises on her skin. I still think of her as beautiful. She says I don't; I say I do. She says I don't, I silently think I do, but I don't contradict her, because who does a man do his best to please, if not his wife?

How was my day, she asks. I tell her that the Nissan ran out of gas again. She asks why I haven't found a solution to the problem yet. I tell her I don't know what else I can do. I have had it checked over. I checked it over myself – not that I know much about cars – and couldn't find any problems. She says that if she was in better shape, she would check it out and she would find the problem. That's true, I say, and it is. Mariana was always able to solve problems; she was very outgoing. It is good to have a wife who complements you.

I set the table, I call María. We all sit down. We do not always eat this well, but today we do: it's like I always say: you can measure the progress of a country by an honest man's dinner table. A man who does not put more food on the table than is his due. And whenever I worry that things are getting worse, I think about my dinner table, how it is today, and how it was a decade ago, and I realize things are not getting worse, they are getting better, they truly are.

We listen to the scraping of forks and plates and spoons. We listen to the sound of mouths chewing. We listen to the table teetering and the sound of a sigh, heaved by one of us as though for all three. We hear the gurgling sound of water trickling down throats as if down a drain. Then Mariana says there has been another phone call.

I feel a twinge in my stomach, but I remain calm – then again, I am always calm. The voice on the telephone is shrill and mocking. I'm tired of trying to get to the bottom of it. We should call the police, I say. No, not the police, Mariana says. María says nothing. I don't know how to change the subject, so I tell the story about the Party official. Mariana smooths her hair, what little she has left, and scolds me.

Afterwards, we sit around the television and watch the news. We pay attention for a while, it is a tradition. We watch a soap opera in which the bad guys are heading for a fall. Then we go to bed. I tuck Mariana in. We quickly manage to doze off, but at some point in the night we are woken by the telephone. One ring, two. Mariana looks at me. Three rings, four. What if it's Diego, she says. What if something's wrong, she says. Nothing. We do nothing. She wants to answer, but I stop her. Nobody knows what a telephone says when no-one answers.

The Daughter

The first time was five months ago, a muffled thud. The human body doesn't sound like a vase shattering. It doesn't sound like a crystal glass. It sounds like a sack of cement, like a thick, heavy dictionary. There was a spot of blood on a corner of the wardrobe, I noticed it straight away. Mamá was lying on the floor, unconscious. There was a gash in her cheek like the hollow in an agave. I did everything you're not supposed to do. I moved her from where she was lying, I tried to put her in a different position. She was a dead weight. She's tall and heavy, and I couldn't get her to her feet. After about three minutes, she started to stir and after a while she came round. We thought it was an isolated incident, but people think a lot of things.

The second time was on the front balcony, while she was watering the plants. The third time was on the balcony at the back. She was hand-washing a few of Diego's old shirts she'd found in an old drawer. That's one of the symptoms, apparently, doing things that don't need doing. I asked what she was doing, washing Diego's shirts she told me. She flashed me the childlike look of a happy or mischievous little girl. Her hands carried on scrubbing at the ridges of the concrete washboard that look like the ribs of an elderly smoker. I asked her why she was washing shirts Diego would never wear and she said that of course Diego would wear these shirts, that he had phoned, that he had been given a furlough next weekend and was coming home.

I didn't want to contradict her, I simply stood and watched. Just then, she hunched over and the strangest thing happened. Her face drained away, seemed to contract, like when you clench a fist, as though everything was drawing back around her nose. Her eyes fell, her forehead and her mouth shriveled and her cheeks began to wither. Then she burst into tears and collapsed.

I don't know where the rest of her body went. Her head grazed the edge of the sink and her forehead slammed into a metal bucket where more shirts and a pile of rags were soaking in cloudy, soapy water. I kept my composure, there was no-one else in the house. There had been no-one else the last two times she fell either. I thought maybe it was something my mother and I shared, that it wasn't really happening. Like a sign, maybe, a code between women. But it was nothing of the kind.

I felt a welling fear and a wave of sadness. Somehow or other, a pair of hands was still scrubbing Diego's shirts. The shirts disintegrated into tatters and Mamá's eyes rolled back into her head. Then my father arrived home from the hotel. He dropped his briefcase and scooped Mamá into his arms. This was a mistake, the rear balcony is very narrow, and it is always piled with junk. It used to drive me mad: the automatic washing machine I bought to replace that old Aurika that had given up the ghost, canvas sacks splotched with red mud, a bag of clothespins, the trash can, a corner crammed with cleaning equipment, a dustpan, a mangle, a new broom and two tatty old ones, a clothes rack still hung with pairs of panties, empty milk bags pinned to the washing line to dry, the steel vegetable crate and, inside, something, I'm not sure what, plantains or cassava or yams or potatoes – not all at the same time, obviously – and a few shriveled strings of garlic.

In that moment, I realized that debris had collected under the washing machine. There were greasy dusters, floor cloths riddled with holes, a plunger, an empty bottle of bleach and another of disinfectant, makeshift plastic funnels and a bucket filled with rusted tools and nails.

Later, we were told that if Mamá had a fall, we should leave her where she was, since moving her might cause more pain. Aches in her muscles and her joints. We rushed her to hospital, EEGs, CAT scans, MRI scans, three weeks of tests before she was discharged with a prescription for Clobazam and Magnesium Valproate which, when the seizures did not abate, was changed to Topiramate and Clonazepam, though these have not done much good either.

The diagnosis states the patient's condition as 'medial temporal lobe epilepsy', brought about, according to the doctors, by the side effects of chemotherapy. Six years ago, Mamá had surgery for endometrial cancer. I knew about it, but Diego didn't. In fact, Diego still thinks Mamá's epilepsy came out of nowhere.

Epilepsy, or seizure disorder, I was told, is characterized by periodic disturbances in electrical brain activity, and in Mamá's case, the area most affected is the temporal lobe. This is the area that processes memory and emotion, controls moods, and is central to hearing and language recognition. Seizures occur more frequently if the patient suffers physical or emotional stress or lack of sleep, though there are other causes.

In Mamá's case, an epileptic crisis or seizure presents by physical collapse accompanied by auras, which can be olfactory, sensory or visual. Then come the tonic-clonic contractions, convulsions that can last from one to three minutes, and are followed by difficulties with speech, coordination and the ability to walk. Mamá doesn't remember what happens during the seizure, nor understand what is being said. This may be followed by confusion, headaches, exhaustion and sleep.

I learned all this by heart, went to visit Diego at the

barracks, explained it to him. I told him he had to come home as soon as he could get leave. He didn't understand, he said, it wasn't possible. He asked if Mamá was a vegetable. Was she a vegetable? Complete bullshit! If – given what I'd told him – the temporal lobes control memories, emotions and moods, surely Mamá would have falls all the time? A person who can't remember is surely agitated or constantly exposed to some imminent emotion, whatever the nature of that emotion. Disgust or joy or sadness or hope or something.

He carried on talking. His outlook on things has always been complicated and confusing. He told me emotion and memory was a daunting subject. I didn't see it like that. I didn't see anything, actually, but what seemed terrible to me were the falls. The jolt, the blood, the illness, the debility and, to some extent, the humiliation. One moment you're here, then something happens and you move into dangerous territory, as though exiled, forced to march from the land of the healthy to the land of the sick. This, surely, was the danger – not memory or emotion.

I told Diego that there was no medical basis for his hypothesis. He insisted that I didn't understand, that if Mamá's seizures were triggered by memory and emotion, then, to save herself, she would have to stupefy herself with drugs. In order not to feel, not to remember. But if a person stops feeling, stops remembering, then what are they, huh? What are they? he said. Hey, I said, hey, what the hell is wrong with you? We were silent for a moment, then Diego said that things were going to get much worse.

And they did. Mamá continued to fall, and she had to give up her job. She forbade any of her pupils or the teachers at her school from coming to visit her. Sometimes, she might have eight seizures in a week, and we could not avoid all of them. The falls are grinding her down, they make her forget the words she needs to say, wants to say, but sometimes she has flashes of memory, like trances, in which she recalls some forgotten incident from her childhood or adolescence or from mine or Diego's childhood. Remembering these things makes her happy, but I know there's nothing to be happy about. I know it's better for her to remember nothing, to have no reason to remember. And then, at some point, things got even worse. We started getting anonymous phone calls and my father fired René from the hotel, which piled more responsibility onto me.

I carried on working as I always had. I told Mamá I wanted to give up my job and stay home to look after her. Mamá told me not to. I know that I can't, but I told her that I wanted to, so she would know. I carry on putting food on the table, splitting myself in three, in four. I don't watch television and, though I'm twenty-three, I don't do anything for fun. Not that I can think of anything that might be fun. The one thing that has changed is that, in recent months, I've developed a reflex reaction to sounds. Even at the hotel, where I know my mother can't be, I flinch at every thud, every creak.

After a number of falls, a body sometimes sounds like a sack of cement, like thick hardback dictionaries, but sometimes it also sounds like a glass or a porcelain vase shattering. I am like a frightened cat. A fork clattering on the floor makes my hair stand on end. But I don't say a word, I bite my tongue. I think I'm a good daughter, and a good person in general.

II

The Son

The root of all happiness depends on sleeping the required number of hours at the time of your choosing. There's no guarantee that you'll be happy if you do sleep properly, but if you don't sleep enough, or sleep at the wrong time, you haven't got a chance. At the core of world angst, at the heart of mediocrity, lies the fact that this shapeless mass of men and women, boys and girls, are daily forced to wake at dawn, at five-thirty, or six, or six-thirty in the morning, and grudgingly go off to work or to school, heads bowed, like cattle daily led to the slaughter, to institutions they despise with every ounce of somnolence and lethargy, yet which they dutifully continue to attend.

The day dawns twisted out of shape. Everything that follows must inevitably go wrong, because what could go right for someone who was woken up in the early hours? Is there any routine more terrible than to hear the alarm clock, reach out to shut it off, get up in the dark, give that sad series of yawns, wipe sleep from our eyes, breakfast on stale bread and a little milk, brush our teeth, change into social prison uniform, all without being totally awake, while the day is still murky and the dawn chill washes over our skin?

The routine of soldiers doing military service in the army is actually worse. Four hours on, four hours off, one day on, one day off. The days without sentry duty we spend at some routine chore, always some backbreaking task, like moving silos of antitank mines, or crates of Kalashnikovs, cleaning and greasing dozens of magazines, whitewashing a large section of the two-and-a-half-meter-high peeling wall that surrounds the barracks, or spending six hours scrubbing the parade ground, or scraping away the caked-on soot in the kitchens.

This is the military sector of town. We are on the outskirts. The surrounding streets are not paved, and only the section of road directly opposite the front gate is lined with ramshackle houses occupied by housewives, coachmen, farriers, silage vendors and emaciated horses and mares that, when not saddled, rest up in dirt-floor stables. The rest of the surrounding wall is ringed by a dense scrubland in which no soldier has ever been lost, a wasteland of few sounds, which makes it seem all the more sinister and terrible at three o'clock in the morning.

There we store crates of rifles, gas masks, landmines, shovels for digging trenches, ammunition of every caliber and a supply of uniforms. Everything we need to equip the populace when war comes, though I think most of the stock has long since corroded. But our mission is to guard it, to protect it. There are two sentry duties: the day shift involves manning the checkpoint, opening the gate for incoming cars, standing to attention and saluting officers; the night shift involves patrolling the central courtyard, guarding the equipment stores and the parking lot. Both day and night, the sentry is required to prowl around the back of the barracks, between the mango trees and the avocados, guarding the weapons cache and the kitchen.

Some soldiers are required to do two years' military service and others, like me, who have been accepted to university, only have to serve one. Lately, the other conscripts have been giving me black looks because I don't have much time left. Today, they were badmouthing me in the barracks. I know because I came back unexpectedly and everyone suddenly shut up. I rested for half an hour after lunch, then went out to start my shift. Sentry duty runs from 8 a.m. to noon, noon to 4 p.m., and so on. In the army, the hours constrict like the jaws of a vice.

Right now I am wearing thick Coloso boots with steel

toecaps that lace up to my calves, an olive-green uniform, *zambrán* belted at the waist, bayonet hanging from the *zambrán,* cap set lightly on my head as though it had just landed there, and I am covering the shift that runs from noon to four o'clock that we soldiers call the 'great yawn'. Even standing, simulating the gait of a sentry digesting his lunch, we can be asleep, and asleep we can carry on walking. Everything we do we do while sleeping, as though we were still inside the same receptacle, but were temporarily a different, more viscous substance.

An officer pulls up in a jeep. I go to the gate. I open it as quickly as possible, doing my best to ensure that the officer notices how efficient I can be opening the front gate, although in fact there is no real way for one soldier to prove that he is more efficient than another when it comes to opening a gate, except, of course, by doing it as quickly as possible, a feat in which, ultimately, the officers take little interest or, let's be honest, no interest whatsoever.

My thighs and the crown of my head are soaked with sweat. I'm sweltering. It's not always like this. I have a body clock that never fails me. In the morning, the light hovers over everything and sometimes there is a breath of wind. There is little heat, day has barely materialized. Later, the light swells and any trace of humidity disappears. By noon, the brightness becomes slightly darker, light does the opposite of what it is supposed to do and shapes lose their contours. Then, for a few seconds, the sun reaches its zenith and the light acquires a liquid quality. It splashes, floods, flows, creates waves, spills over, drowns. By now, the sun has finally become an iron sun, hard, that rolls like a rock, and upon this bed we rest.

But day is routine to an old soldier. It is night that tests the strength of our mental health. In the early hours, contrary to what you might think, every object is awake and every one of them is watching. A soldier can listen to what the walls and the columns are saying to him, but he must never answer. The most basic solution is masturbation. My quota is to jerk off three times per shift. I always leave the first one until at least two hours into my sentry duty, so I can get to the mid-point without a dopamine rush. Knowing you have three hours left and three *pajas* in reserve is not the same as knowing you've got three hours' sentry duty left and you've already wasted one. The second option means you've got more time reserved for yourself.

There are other techniques: overcoming your fear of the night or of the darkness, shaking off the fear of noises, realizing that noises are your friends, that your real enemy is silence, welcoming pleasant memories, driving out bad memories and, if you don't have many pleasant memories, keep your mind blank and take every minute as it comes, shift after shift, until the war comes.

There is also a secret weapon that every soldier has depending on his circumstances and the kind of person he is, a weapon nobody ever talks about, a devious act each of us perpetrates only in absolute solitude. If you manage to discover this secret weapon, everything is more bearable. So, for example, with all my duties here, I don't have time to think about my mother. Busy as I am doing nothing, I don't have space to think about much else.

The Mother

Armando sips a little water and avoids my gaze. He doesn't like to be criticized, but I'm not *criticizing*, I'm just explaining something he clearly can't see. Over dinner, between mouthfuls, he told me a Party official had asked him to replace a barman and a cashier at the hotel with two people from the reserve staff. He told me he'd refused. I said the Party official was obviously trying to promote two men he was colluding with to steal from the hotel. He said that this was precisely why he'd refused. I told him everyone would assume that he was conspiring with the two employees he refused to replace, that common theft, rather than any other motive, would be seen as the reason he refused.

Principle, he told me, I refused on principle. I cannot allow people to steal, he said. María stares down at her food. Alright then, on principle, I said to him, and Armando launched into the story of Che Guevara, how once he refused a bicycle that a factory foreman had given him for his daughter. These bicycles, Armando said Che said, belong to the State, not to you.

I've heard the story too many times. I don't know whether Armando made it up or whether it's true. It's a story that makes my head ache. I heard it a year and a half ago when he was transferred. At the time, Armando was working in the provincial delegation of the Ministry of Tourism and they appointed him manager of the hotel. He wanted to fire María in case he was accused of nepotism, but María had been working at the hotel long before Armando was appointed, so there wasn't much he could do. In fact, some of his colleagues – Armando's colleagues – arranged to give María a job as restaurant manager. Behind his back. Armando was furious. I hadn't wanted María to give up university either, but she was happier this way. All things considered, we didn't really have much choice. For me, it was a relief.

Then María met René and they became friends. I thought they might get together – wanted them to, even – but it never happened. Even so, for some reason, René started to help out the family. Then Armando took up the hotel job and, since he already knew René, picked him from all the men in the driving pool to be his driver. René told me he didn't want to do it. With the greatest respect, I don't want to be the manager's personal driver, he said. But he wasn't referring to the manager. He was referring to Armando. I understand, *hijo,* I said, as I handed him a cup of coffee. I remember it clearly. A steaming cup of coffee that René grasped between two fingers on which there were still traces of oil, and engine grease under his nails, as the afternoon light streamed in from my balcony and pooled in the hollow of his hand.

We finish eating. María goes to her room, claiming she is tired. Armando washes the dishes and I go watch TV. The telephone rings and Armando rushes to answer. It's for me. I signal to say I'm not here. It's a former pupil wanting to know, worrying about me. To be honest, I don't want to talk to any of them. I spent twenty-five years educating children that life went on to destroy. I'd rather have devoted myself to my own children. But they're all in the past. Those I taught and those I didn't.

Around midnight, Armando closes the windows, throws the bolt on the door and we go to bed. In the early hours, the telephone rings and I jolt awake. Armando stops me answering. Sparks are flashing inside my head. I clench my jaw and shuffle closer to him. It's cold and I'm alone and dawn is breaking. Although I slept, I don't feel as though I rested.

Armando and María are heading to work. I don't feel like doing anything, I rummage through the drawers, change the bedsheets and lie down again. My body is like a country I sometimes visit. I've spent months waiting on the wrought iron benches bolted around the ring roads of my ears and no-one has come, no car, no horse and cart, no messenger.

I have traversed the arch of my brow, thinking it was the main street of the city, expecting that there would be rumbling buses, traffic lights and paperboys on every corner, until an ancient red dust settled over my eyes. Rocks rolled and tumbled with a crash. I swam long miles out to sea, through dark waters. I dived as many fathoms as my lungs would allow. It seemed to me that here, in these depths, something was lurking, burrowing into the seabed, small blind lobsters, delicate, timid creatures, terrified and misshapen in their panic. But I could not make them out.

What exactly am I, if I already know I am not this flesh? Where is my house, my home? What part of me can they kill that does not ache? What part would hurt like a distant relative? What part would hurt like a family member and what part would hurt as though it were me? I am not a corpuscle moving through my own body from crown to toe. I lie quite still, curled up behind some specific zone, trying to make sure that death does not find me. I look at my hand, move it, and it seems independent of me. I understand that I am not this hand, that I am located somewhere outside it.

I get up, go into the kitchen and drink some water. Someone's talking on TV, though I don't remember turning it on. But I don't turn it off. A teacher is giving a lecture in English. I stare at the ceiling. I see shapes, but I can't quite make them out. I see blotches. I close my eyes.

Still I see shapes, still I see blotches and still I can't make them out. The teacher's words are music to my ears. He has a gentle voice and, within that voice, that last inevitable deadlock of those languages that are not one's own. This is what I am inside my body. I am its language. Nothing more.

What is the study of chemistry? I hear the teacher ask. There is silence. Chemicals, one of the pupils seems to say. Chemicals? says the teacher. And then he says no, and then, I think, he says that the study of chemistry is not chemicals. Technically, chemistry is the study of matter, he says, but I prefer to think of it as the study of changes.

I am so calm that I cannot feel my heartbeat. I go into the sitting room – my English isn't good enough, so I have to read the subtitles. Pay attention, he says, electrons change their levels of energy. My heart is still beating. I know this because otherwise I wouldn't be able to think it wasn't beating. Molecules change their bonds, he says. His voice is serious, I sense that this man enjoys teaching. Elements combine and are transformed into compounds. This is life itself, isn't it, he asks. I nod. This *is* life itself. It is the constant, he says, the cycle. Solution, dissolution, again and again. It is growth, decomposition and then transformation, he says. Then he adds something that I don't have time to read.

I'd like to have sex with this teacher, hear his foreign voice trickling into my ears.

The Father

I stayed in my seat when the car stalled, the seatbelt digging into my belly. I looked in the rear-view mirror. There were lots of cars coming behind, a huge flatbed truck carrying containers and, in the distance, a bicycle appeared carrying a man and a little girl. It looked as though the man was her father and was taking the little girl to school, though I don't know if I saw this at first glance, probably not.

At first glance, I think all I saw behind the truck was the deserted road for the ribbon of asphalt that it is, the concrete scar that all roads are. I don't think the father and girl appeared till much later. Either way, I stayed in the driver's seat for as long as necessary, the seatbelt digging into my belly, until the father and the little girl appeared in my rear-view mirror, a barely visible speck, something so far away it was impossible to know exactly what it might be, but which, as it approached, resolved into a father and his daughter. They cycled past, she wearing a primary school uniform and a red bandana, her lunch bag dangling from the handlebar. They were not talking and yet they still seemed to have a perfect father-daughter relationship.

I remembered a particular day, a long time ago. This was during the 'difficult years', and I had not gone to work. I was suffering from a low-grade fever, a slight malaise. I was rocking in my chair in the sitting room and Mariana came over and sat on my lap, with that fusty smell of hers. Back then, everyone had a fusty smell. It was almost noon. Mariana had come in from the kitchen, her skin and her sweat soured by the smells of cooking and of lard. A thick oily sheen covered her arms and neck, strands of hair were plastered to her breasts.

She kissed me, looked at me for a moment, then went back to her chores. At the time, I could roam the house with my eyes closed and recognize everything by the sound it made, the internal workings of this machine that was home. The fridge door being opened. A stove burner being turned on, gas hissing. Mariana striking a match, then going out onto the rear balcony and rummaging in the vegetable box. Then she did nothing, waiting for the frying pan to heat up, probably staring at the burnt floating specks floating in cooking oil recycled for the umpteenth time. Then she put something into the pan, took a plate from the dish rack, opened a plastic lunchbox, and then Mariana came and stood in the doorway between the dining room and the sitting room, holding the plastic container.

She looked at me again, said my name. I folded the newspaper I'd taken from my briefcase. I said: I'm doing what I can. Mariana said: Think about it. I said: I don't need to think about it. I said: Please, let's drop the subject. She said: I don't think you're being very fair. I said: Give me the lunchbox, I'll go.

Mariana did not respond. I took the plastic container from her hand, found a bag and put it inside. I strode down the street and my fever gradually faded. I didn't notice I had arrived at the school until the commotion roused me from my daydream. A little boy raced past, bumped into me, stumbled and almost fell. Three steps further on, his playmate caught up with him. They were laughing and panting. Their untucked shirt tails were as grubby as their pants. I called after them in my sternest voice. Tuck in your shirts, I said. One of the boys apologized. The other grumbled but eventually obeyed. He unbuckled his belt and pushed his shirt into his pants, although the shirt was short and would probably quickly come untucked again.

Eleven, my daughter was at the time. I walked through the entrance hall, crossed the playground and came to her classroom. She was sitting at one of the desks at the back of the room. She was writing in a copybook, with books scattered all around her. I kissed her forehead. She was surprised to see me, which was unsurprising. I had never been the one to bring her lunch. I tried to straighten her hair, but she pushed my hand away, as though I was bothering her. She took out the lunchbox and made a space for it among the books.

She stirred the egg into the rice. She pricked the yolk, and I saw the yellow ooze out. My daughter shoveling this mixture onto her spoon, deft and contented. She cut the banana into slices. I looked carefully at her lunchbox, almost surprised. I knew exactly what her lunch would be, but I had not expected to see her eating rice and eggs and ripe banana, as though I harbored a secret hope that, on my way here, a conjuror might have magically transformed the ingredients in the container.

Having sliced the banana, she barely touched it, saving it for later. My daughter was learning to master the art of scarcity. A grain of rice clung to the corner of her lips as she swallowed in silence. She loaded the spoon and brought it to her mouth, happy. Then she lifted her head and I saw her face, an image that would never fade, one that I would remember as I was sitting in the Nissan ten years later, the spoon suspended halfway between the lunchbox and her mouth, loading as much as she could onto the spoon and yet trying to leave some behind, wanting to sate her hunger and yet wanting to prolong this meal as much as possible. My daughter chewed, and seeing me looking at her, she laid a hand on my shoulder and waited until she had swallowed. Only then, with

42

a pungent whiff of fried egg, did her delicate voice burst forth: Is something wrong, Papá?

I carried on with my recollections, an extensive, almost day-by-day review, thumbing through the book of my life, the jobs I had had, my children growing up, my convictions strengthening, the people I was forced to face down, the familiar progress, the collective resistance, the day I started work at the hotel, my driver's betrayal, in short, everything. Until I reached this morning when the Nissan once against left me halfway down the road. I decided to go home and that is what I did. I crossed the road and from the opposite footpath I hitched a lift. I stopped at a shop in the neighborhood, took the liberty just this once of treating myself to a six-pack of beer and carried on walking.

When I got home and opened the door, Mariana was lying under the dining room table, covered in blood. At first glance I couldn't tell what she had broken. For a second, I stared at her – one of her legs was twitching. After a moment, I got her to her feet, cleaned her up best I could and carried her to bed. I called the hotel and said: I'm not coming in. I informed them of the location of the Nissan. I opened a beer and went out to drink it on the balcony. On the television, a chemistry professor was giving lessons. I thought about pipettes, densimeters, test tubes. The professor was speaking English. Average height, Caucasian, with reddish hair and mustache. He was wearing spectacles, beige polyester pants and a shirt with yellow and green stripes, but in pale tones.

He was discussing chirality, which is no more, he explained, than the ability of an object to be superposed onto what scientists call its mirror image. Meaning its double. The left, the professor said, referring to a pair of hands, is equal to the right. Identical, but opposite. The professor was trying to explain to his students that organic compounds can behave like hands. The students seemed to understand the analogy; some were scribbling in their notebooks. Except that, although they look the same, the professor said, gesturing to the diagram of a compound on the blackboard, they do not always behave in the same way. He mentioned thalidomide, its right enantiomer, and how it was prescribed to pregnant women because it alleviated morning sickness.

I finished the first beer, opened a second and drained it. I could not bear to listen to much more of this. If, by mistake, he explained, the left enantiomer of thalidomide was given to a pregnant woman, her child would be born with terrible physical defects. And he added: which is exactly what happened in the nineteen fifties. Children were born with eyes in their forehead and brains like shriveled raisins.

I filled a bucket with water, there was an aluminum beaker floating in it, and I set about watering the plant. After the fourth beer, flashes began to flicker like a defective x-ray machine, and in the darkness between the flashes, I no longer saw the static image of my apartment, its walls and furniture, but glimpsed what was hidden within that image.

What did it take for this to happen? Not simply alcohol. There were probably many other extenuating and aggravating circumstances, but these extenuating and aggravating circumstances were now common to everyone and I did not dare use them in my defense. This was my day off and I was tending my garden.

The Daughter

According to Mamá, whoever is phoning says I'm a dyke. They say: Your daughter is a lesbian. They say: Your husband is a communist informant. They say: Your daughter is a pervert; this is the girl you raised. They say: Your son is going to kill your husband. They say: This is your last year on earth. The voice, according to Mamá, is shrill, impersonal, the voice of someone who knows. The voice sometimes cackles and adds: I'm inside your head, you dyke, inside your head.

Mamá says that Migdalia is making the calls, but I don't think she really believes that. She says it to have something to say, to have someone to blame. The idea of not having someone to blame is becoming unbearable. I know for a fact it's not Migdalia. I'll come home from work, see Migdalia chatting to a neighbor in the street, go inside only for Mamá to scream that she has just had another call. So it can't possibly be Migdalia. But Mamá insists it is.

I understand her fixation. It's unfair, but I understand it. Migdalia was her best friend. Although, actually, when it comes down to it, according to my very personal criteria, there's no such things as a best friend, no-one is anyone's friend, everyone is alone. Migdalia and Mamá were alone too, but, for a time, they pretended not to be. A long time, in fact. Years spent feigning friendship, love, understanding.

They are neighbors, both secondary school teachers, both working at the same school. Migdalia teaching Physics and Mamá Spanish. They used to go to work together and come home together. Each carrying a handbag, each wearing a gray or black skirt and a print blouse. They gossiped and plotted together. They shared secrets and inanities. It seemed to me that they were always willing to listen to each other. People say that's the meaning of friendship. Listening to a friend, paying attention, even – or especially – when what the friend is saying does not concern you.

But then, two years ago, televisions and telephones were allocated to each neighborhood committee, one television and one telephone to be shared by an entire building. Neighbors vied for them based on their qualities and their merits. People said they were a reward for behavior; actually, they were the opposite: the seeds of destruction. Rumors quickly began to circulate, and that was the end of everything, because stairwell gossip is a cancer. You start to hear it and day by day you watch as it spreads, and the whole building becomes like a moldering potato rotting in the vegetable crate.

Migdalia stopped coming round, or did so only when she had to. Sometimes she visited just to keep up appearances, the same reason Mamá still visited her sometimes. She would ask to borrow a cup of sugar, a bottle of cold water or some ice, and Mamá would ask for a few onions, a head of garlic, who knows what. But all this went on because they didn't know how to live any other way. By that point, their friendship was like a car that continues to coast for a few meters after the engine is turned off. How can a friendship break down between two people who will carry on living next door to each other forever, who will carry on seeing each other, bumping into each other to their dying day? I think they reacted in the most cowardly way possible: by stopping talking to each other. I think they stopped talking at precisely the moment when they needed to talk, but I don't know, the honest truth is I don't really know. All I know is that, when the time to patch things up came and went, they were looking the other way.

Then came the fateful day and I felt that, even if we were awarded the television, it was already too late, the damage was done. I was twenty at the time. Diego, fifteen. What difference would a television make at that stage? Everyone in the building gathered in the street at eight-thirty, after the news bulletin. We gathered around the steps. A flag fluttered from the balcony. The delegate tasked with explaining the situation asked us to come closer. He stood in the middle, clutching a sheaf of papers. We were a peaceable building, as far as that goes. Why had we been favored, I wondered? Every family that did not have a television or a telephone longed for a television and a telephone. I didn't, Diego didn't, but Mamá did. There was so much fear that every face was frozen, as though set in plaster, as the delegate spoke. This balm that was a television and a telephone, this – I don't know – this privilege, was about to destroy the solidarity that poverty had managed to foster, the bond of penury.

The television and the telephone would be allocated to the family unit that had accumulated most credits in the various five-yearly assessments. Assessments determined which family was least introverted, which had the most gregarious members, those most likely to greet their neighbors or call to them from their balcony. The reason for their conversation did not matter: it could be because they were draining the water tank, or because you needed some salt or a bar of soap. This was an important point. Which families were most in need? Which needed to ask more of their neighbors? It was important to ensure that all families lacked something; this was a guarantee of altruism.

Families were also classified according to which had the poorest ancestors. Which had most suffered throughout history? The credits accumulated by the living were not enough. If a family could prove that a great-grandparent had died of starvation during some nineteenth-century redistribution of land, or something of the kind, that family had tickets for the jackpot.

We'd heard stories of how the allocation worked from other buildings. A neighbor would nominate someone. Another neighbor would nominate someone else. After that, although people tried to remain civil, the battle between the supporters of one or the other neighbor gradually escalated. The nominees tried to stay above the fray but, obviously, each was feverishly keeping a tally of friends and enemies. At some point, someone would make an offensive remark, someone else would insult them back, and before long everyone's dirty laundry was being aired in public, as though the neighbors had spent their whole lives silently passing judgment so that they could settle scores on the day the television and the telephone finally arrived.

There were reports of fights at some neighborhood meetings, hair-pulling among the women, brawls among the men. But the quarrels where people actually came to blows were not very serious. In most cases, neighbors patched up their differences and some made their television available to everyone in the building. The telephone had previously fulfilled this function. It was allocated to a particular family, but the family had to draw up a schedule of when the device was available to their neighbors, preferably late at night. Although in our building, nobody ever wanted to use it and even now, no-one uses it. Why? So there was no bloodshed. So that it was all kept inside, like a spreading bruise that became infected, silently eating away at us.

The delegate concluded his speech. We all looked at

each other in silence until someone loudly cleared his throat. Good, said the delegate, let's have a nomination. No-one pointed out that our building was different to all the others, even though we had been through the same things, but it was. No-one spoke, no-one said a word, five minutes of communal silence. People who had spent their lives talking each other's ears off were suddenly dumb as fenceposts. A nomination, the delegate said again. Migdalia spoke up: Mariana and Armando, she said.

In how many buildings would a rival nominate her opponent? Well, Migdalia did just that. There was an unwritten rule observed by candidates of genuine merit, that they shouldn't nominate anyone but wait for others to put forward nominations. Some people are more worthy than others, and everyone always knows whose role it is to propose, and whose to wait to be nominated. Migdalia was not supposed to propose, she was supposed to wait to be nominated. Instead she nominated Mamá.

My father told Diego to take down the flag. Everyone went back to their apartment. Migdalia and Mamá haven't spoken to each other in the last three years. They haven't uttered a word to each other. It didn't seem to bother Mamá, not until she started to get ill, but I know that Migdalia is not the person making the anonymous calls. Actually, we all know. I suspect Mamá actually knows who is doing it but doesn't want to say.

I wonder about that, although to tell the truth, I wonder about a lot of other things. Where Mamá's illness came from, for example. Whether I enjoy my job. Whether I like having to shoulder the responsibility for everything at home. What my parents were like before they were my parents? But, most of all, the big question, the million-dollar question, the question that has haunted me my whole life, one that sounds preposterous yet somehow isn't: Why do neither of them eat chicken, in any form, and why have they never talked about it?

Never means never, right? They never eat chicken, and they never talk about the fact that they don't. Never.

III

The Son

So, we used to eat on the floor. We didn't have a table. I know it sounds unbelievable, because everyone's got a table, but there was no table in the house, that's how poor we were. It didn't bother me. I would have been – what? – four? five years old? Life was a party, nothing mattered. I believed what anyone would have believed at that age, that the world came predesigned without tables in dining rooms, that the world, at its most basic, lacked certain things, and that people in every home in the country ate the same way we did, with a tablecloth spread on the floor – ours was lime green with stains where various things had been spilled – and four cushions that served as chairs.

Later, there was a table, I think we brought it over from my grandmother's old house, in perfect condition, though over time it began to wobble. I don't know why, if there was a table in grandmother's house, we spent months and probably years eating off the floor, but Armando must have wanted it that way, it must have been part of his Spartan plan, his frugal plan, his new man plan.

There were a lot of things we didn't have. I never had roller skates. I never had a bicycle. I never had a birthday party. I never had a Nintendo. In the grand scheme of things this was no big deal, but in my neighborhood, where other boys, whose fathers also worked in the tourist industry but stole with appropriate abandon, never wanted for anything, it was a big deal. I was the black sheep of the block. That said, bicycles and roller skates and birthday parties aren't essential. I know that, I accept it. But TV. We never had a TV. How can I explain? How can I explain what it meant to come home from school at the age of eight, or nine, or ten, and have nothing to turn on, when every other house had one? What it was like to stare at the empty space in the middle of the living room where the TV should have been, playing children's programs?

This is the cornerstone of my personality and I stand up for who I am, a kid who grew up watching cartoons in neighbor's sitting rooms, a kid who had to peek through the railings of other people's windows, or stand on a step-ladder, or watch through a doorway. I was top of my class, my parents knew it, everyone knew it. And they never rewarded me, they never even thought to. OK, I wasn't aware of it at the time. I thought that my parents gave me everything they could, but now I realize that's not true, that they could have done more, especially Armando. I don't understand why my mother didn't just get a divorce. What was the point of staying with this ridiculous, old fogey of a husband and, in the process, sacrificing her kids' childhood?

I was in first grade and the teachers would take me out of the classroom, stand me in front of a class of kids who were two or three years older than me, and have me recite multiplication tables, or the postulates of Euclidean geometry. A line is the shortest distance between two points, I would say, or a circle can be drawn using any center and any radius, or any segment can be extended indefinitely in a straight line, which is the postulate that particularly interests me today, or two lines are parallel if they never intersect, I would say, although I now know this is false because at some moment, at some point, everything intersects, the line, the curve and the void, and my teachers would look at me proudly, unlike the older pupils, obviously, who hated me, but my teachers praised me and applauded me, I was their prize pupil, their blue-eyed boy, and they must have said so to my parents. It goes without saying that my parents never helped me with my homework because they didn't need to, I worked things out by myself, my ability with numbers was proven, it was well-known, but my parents never rewarded me, they knew, but they did nothing, maybe they felt they *deserved* a son like me, but looking back now it is perfectly clear that they didn't deserve me at all.

What would I have asked of them? Some recognition. The only advice I ever got from my atheist father was this: the Three Wise Men don't exist (in Cuba, it's the Three Wise Men who bring children presents at Christmas). It's a pernicious piece of propaganda, he told me, a lie designed to confuse, alienate and stupefy children. He was right. Educating me to reject the lies that the rabble take for facts was a good thing. But I'd like to draw attention to two things.

The first is that if a father is going to deprive you of the Three Wise Men, it is his responsibility to take their place, not leave you orphaned at the age of six or seven, the way Armando did me. He turned off the light and I found myself alone in the darkened room of my intelligence, with nothing to rebut him, like a straight line fired across the immensity of space that, no matter how far it goes, encounters no-one, even when the mysterious laws of the universe suggest it could and should happen, companionship and loneliness contracted to a single point.

I'm not trying to say anything in particular by that, but I was the kind of kid who used to stand in front of the bathroom mirror – we were lucky to have a bathroom mirror – and stare at himself for minutes on end, the boy that I was astonished at the thought that was being reflected was him, completely alien to himself, attempting to understand, to assimilate what was being reflected and how what was being reflected was him rather than anything else, or was all that he was, all the infinite daydreams, the crazy ideas, the tender thoughts, the dizzying accumulation of fundamental trivialities that a man is even as a child, all contained within this reflected face in which, with reason, I did not completely recognise myself.

And the second is that later, when I was ten or eleven, Armando did try to replace the Three Wise Men with his own ideology and that was worse, because he achieved his goal. I was launched onto the meat-grinding machine that is thinking like your father, taking on the passions and rages of your father. And all this without a TV. The TV never appeared. I began to be more disciplined in my reading, though I still didn't really enjoy it. I read every night, I read the books Armando gave me, the book of stories about Che Guevara that tells how Che refused the gift of a bicycle for his daughter, because bicycles belong to the State, to the People, not to any particular individual.

I asked Armando why, if bicycles were for everyone and not for individuals, they made bicycles for individuals to ride? Why didn't they make a gigantic bicycle that we could all get on and pedal together, millions of pedals moving at the same time, all riding in the same direction? That's what we are doing, Armando said, we are all riding one great bicycle, son, we are pedaling the bicycle of justice. And then I remember my mother – who looked like she wasn't listening when obviously she was, the way mothers do, never missing a trick – saying: Oh, of course we're all pedaling, but the chain has fallen off.

She laughed at her own joke. Armando did not laugh, far from it – he didn't take it well. Later Armando, indefatigable, continued inoculating me with his positive energy, his moral code, his inexhaustible optimism, injecting me with a radioactive material that, on contact with the real world, simply exploded like acid in a burst battery and was transformed into frustration. I'm eighteen years old but I feel like an old man. This was what Armando was really injecting me with. And, yes, you endure the contradictions and convictions of your parents. It is this disconnect that gives you life, until you are shaking with rage.

My mother's illness, in the end, is a fish hook that she has cast to bring me back to them. I realized this from the very beginning. In primary school, I would wait desperately for her at the end of the day. Her slim, sheltering figure would round the corner, rescue me and take me home. A memory that tries to resurface in the early hours of sentry duty, which I quickly brush aside. My mother's kiss at the school gate. Her hug at four in the afternoon. Her questions about my homework, her delicate conversation, warm and tender as a glove, her innocuous scoldings. When it came to high school, I wanted to attend the school where she taught, and she wanted that too, but Armando wouldn't allow it.

Thus began my exile at various secondary schools and boarding schools, rarely coming home, barely either a child or an adolescent. After that, I was drafted by the army. I spent several months in the military sector, sleeping in a hostel on days when I had leave, but my sister came to visit and said to me: Mamá is ill. I refused to believe her, but I went home anyway. And I sat at the table. From the start, the tension was palpable. The background hum of the television. My mother was more condescending than ever, despite her pale, gaunt appearance. Armando tried to initiate conversations he couldn't follow through. I tried to be equally communicative. My sister hardly said a word, but her face maintained a mute rictus of harmony and pleasure intended to let us know how happy she was that we were all together again.

5 8

After the meal, I tried to ease the tension, to break the stilted formality, because, at the end of the day, this was my family, so I told my sister a story I'd heard from one of the soldiers in the unit. Then, suddenly, everything seemed pathetic, ridiculous, utterly ridiculous but real, atrociously real, and, unable to believe what was happening, I got up and went to bed and, early next morning, reported back to the military sector and took the 8 a.m. shift at sentry post number two, and as I wandered through a thick tangle of avocado trees, I saw myself as a little boy again: we were heading to the beach in my father's first Lada, the car he had before the Nissan, before everything, on one of the few occasions that Armando agreed to drive us to the beach, if not the only one.

It was Sunday, the beach and the resort hotels were no more than twenty kilometers from the town, my sister and I were playing in the back seat, joking and singing songs that, despite the difference in our ages, we both enjoyed, maybe because my sister was always a little young for her age and I was a little old for mine, and then, after a while, my sister fell asleep, and I turned around and gazed out the rear windscreen at the road, the way it rolled away from the back seat of the car, the way I stared out, with my chin propped on my hands, the way the wind whipped at my hair.

Somehow, I thought as I manned the sentry post, I am still in that car. Somehow, my parents have parked, got out, put on their swimsuits and gone down to the beach, or to bronze themselves on the sand, and I am still traveling with my sister, in a car, an old-fashioned car, but my sister is asleep, not because she is tired, but because she doesn't want to and perhaps can't see what I am seeing. I searched for goodness outside, but found only dissipation.

The Mother

Things were hard for everyone and they were terrible for teachers, although those of us with experience, those who'd made their mark, were a little better off. No more than a centimeter, but during the 'Special Period', a centimeter was an infinity. Those of us who lived through it, we know. There were parents who gave Migdalia and me whatever they could. They would come up to us like people who are not in need and are not about to take no for an answer and say: Look, we would just like to give you this, *maestra,* we want to thank you for everything you're doing for our son. Teachers deserted the profession en masse to work in the tourist industry. Only the two of us and a handful of others stayed behind. The parents who, in spite of everything, still wanted their children to have an education, appreciated our ability to stand firm.

Sometimes, we would go home with half a liter of cooking oil, sometimes with a packet of *croquetas* or a piece of chorizo. Sometimes a basket of eggs, or a few pounds of sugar or rice. Sometimes, if we were really lucky, a kilo of tomatoes or cucumbers or, by some miracle, a few ripe avocados. I don't know where people got the food. Nobody knows, to be honest. Now, thinking back, all we remember is a cycle of hunger, a state of siege in which there was nothing, an emptiness in every plate, an emptiness in the shops, an emptiness in the freezer compartment of the fridge, an emptiness in the fields and in the factories, and an emptiness, larger than all the rest, in our hearts and in our stomachs.

But it seems clear that, in the end, this emptiness could not have been as big or as absolute as we remember, because if we are to go by what we remember, none of us should have survived. The inevitable outcome of the abject poverty we remember would have been a hideous pyre of corpses, decomposing bodies, droning flies. But that isn't what happened. We are what we are, granted; crippled, yes; mutilated, yes; shattered, yes; but alive. It doesn't matter what our memories say, there was food. Energy infused from somewhere. I believe it came from within, from abject poverty itself.

Cells contain vesicles that, in extreme situations, break down part of their cellular matter in order to maintain cellular energy levels. There is a sort of molecular brake that prevents cellular autophagy from veering out of control, upsetting the balance between the energy consumed by the starving cell and the energy it generates via the process, resulting in infection and, in turn, the failure of the cellular emergency plan, a delicate system refined by millions of years of evolution. Something like this is what happened.

We scratched a living as best we could – Migdalia and I and a handful of others. Sometimes, as we walked home, we wondered why people kept giving us things when they had nothing to give. There was a popular song at the time that people danced to. The hero was an old stewing hen no-one wanted to eat at first, but later everyone was fighting over. It was a song by Los Van Van called 'Que le den candela' - 'Stick him on the barbecue,' and I'm afraid we carried on dancing to it because, despite all the families raising chickens in cages by the heat of a lightbulb, this song was the only place where we could not only find a chicken, but actually eat one. At first despised, and later coveted by all, the chicken ended as soup.

One afternoon, against all odds, in the midst of this mass hallucination about imaginary chickens, a mother gave me some chicken breasts carefully wrapped in a nylon bag. Her son was one of the least gifted in the class and I usually treated him with contempt but, even so, when his mother gave me the chicken breasts, he seemed to be smiling. I thought the boy hated me, the way stupid children hate their teachers, but this particular pupil did not hate me, at least not in that moment, he seemed happy. Thanks to him and to his family, his teacher would be able to eat that night.

It was 4.20 p.m., the school gates were closing, and the boy's mother hurriedly pressed the bag into my hands. People were constantly stealing, and constantly sharing out the spoils, a practice that carries on to this day, but these particular breasts, sliced from a chicken the pupil's mother had spent months patiently, carefully fattening in her back yard, had been filleted explicitly for me.

Such theories wouldn't flourish until later. That afternoon, the pupil's mother merely handed me a nylon bag, I simply took it and thanked her politely, and the only thing that aroused my curiosity was a sogginess, the thawed state of the chicken breasts. I didn't even wait for Migdalia. I needed to cook them before some catastrophe could occur. We lived in a world of routine power cuts and I had nowhere to store the package.

María was in the sitting room, playing with pieces of junk, fabrics, plastic, the arms and heads of broken dolls. Diego was coloring pictures in a book with a pencil, since he had no crayons, so that all the animals and plants were gray, indistinguishable, as if in a bleak winter. My mother-in-law, who was still alive, would come and look after them during the day.

I immediately changed my clothes, put on a pair of slippers and started cooking. The walls were covered in soot and the apartment was falling to pieces. I had to make the most of the daylight. I marinated the chicken breasts in salt and lemon, something simple. The lemons gave very little juice. I took down the rice as I worked. The chicken breasts had a soft golden color, it seemed almost a pity to eat them, to consume something so beautiful only once.

I told my children that we would be having chicken for dinner. For breakfast, they had only had half a glass of milk and a piece of toast with oil and salt, for lunch a bowl of sweetened cornmeal, but they weren't hungry. Their developing bodies had already learned moderation. Neither of them showed any interest. Thinking about it, I couldn't remember them ever eating chicken when they were old enough to remember. And if, by chance, they had ever eaten it, they had no reason to remember it as anything special.

When Armando arrived home, he came into the kitchen with me, still in his work uniform. We both knew this was a special occasion. We had salad vegetables for the weekend, but he suggested that perhaps we might have them tonight. Eat well for a day rather than badly for a week. Of course, I said, of course, darling, let's have the salads. What is there? he asked. Some green beans and an avocado, I said. Alright, he said, let's do it. We prepared the green beans, sliced the avocado and drizzled it with a little oil, cooked the chicken breasts with slices of an onion we found among the parings as we rooted through the vegetable box. This was our lucky day.

We laid out the tablecloth, sat on our cushions and served the food. Larger portions for the children, as we always did. Some families – and I'm not criticizing them, actually, I think they were right – did things differently. The parents, who were responsible for finding the food, ate more because if they did not keep up their strength and some illness laid them up in bed, who would feed their children? I was in favor of adopting this approach, but Armando refused. The children come first, he would always say.

We started eating. There was more color on the plates than usual. Armando looked at me and I looked at him, wide-eyed, and we heard a wild peal of laughter coming from our mouths. We mingled the intense yellow-green of the avocado, the pale gold of the chicken, the white of the rice, the translucent onions, a whole festival of colors and flavors in a single forkful. Eleven incomparable forkfuls, my plate lasted. Armando finished before me.

When we looked up, we saw the children playing with their food. Pushing it around their plates, toying with the rice, mashing the avocado. It was not funny. All this food, for one day, right in front of them, cooked, served, and here they were letting it go to waste. I collected the empty plates and piled them in the sink. I drank a glass of water, smoked a cigarette, stared out the window. The neighborhood looked as though it had been colored with my son's pencil. I paced the apartment, I gave them some time. Then I said: What? Are you not going to eat? They sat in silence. Don't be afraid, I said, just tell me, are you not going to eat? They were used to us forcing them to eat. I want sweet cornmeal, said Diego. María nodded. I want cornmeal too.

You don't like the chicken? I said. They didn't say anything. Is that what it is, I said, you don't like the chicken? Answer me, I said. Not really, María said. That's fine, I said. Their faces lit up when I said this. Don't eat the chicken, I said. We're not going to force you if you don't want to, are we Armando? We're not going to force them, Armando said. If they don't want to eat, they don't have to, he said. That's right, I said, we won't make them. Do you want your cornmeal now? I asked. More self-assured, Diego said he wanted it later. No problem, son, I said, we have cornmeal. When you want it, you just tell me, I said.

They went on sitting on the cushions, legs crossed. In fact, they weren't really hungry for anything, except perhaps a glass of milk before they went to bed, but there was no milk left that day. They didn't like cornmeal, but they liked chicken even less. They had said they wanted cornmeal because to them it seemed the easiest way out. Alright, I said, take your plates into the kitchen.

I folded the tablecloth. The children went back to their games. María picked up the broken toys and Diego his coloring book. I took one of the plates, Armando took the other. I don't remember us saying a word. We went out onto the rear balcony. In silence. Outside, the sun was beginning to set. The taste of the fried chicken breast. We didn't think we were doing anything wrong.

The Father

This is the dream. A dark figure approaches in the night, blacker than the inky blackness. The man is wearing an overcoat and his face cannot be seen, even if he turns toward me. He moves to the center of the scene, slips a hand into his black pocket, shades of darkness, takes out a black key, slots it into the black car door, slides into the driver's seat and adjusts the black ribbon of the seatbelt. He grips the steering wheel and spends a few seconds warming up the engine, which must be purring. I say 'must be' because there is no sound. Then the car pulls away. I cannot make out the driver's features. I glance in every mirror, but nothing. He is a mystery, his appearance is closed to me. Blackness against blackness and speed.

The journey begins along a hard, smooth road, the never-ending journey along the lonely avenue of dreams, first at sixty, then at eighty, within the applicable speed limit, but then at a hundred, a hundred and twenty, at a hundred and forty, even a hundred and eighty, and at some point along the way, I become the driver, who is and is not me, because it is as though we are still two things, both of them at the wheel, the driver and me, superposed.

My heart beats faster, my stomach lurches into my mouth. We pass trees and fields and electric pylons, until the road narrows to become a single point. Length becomes compressed, the horizon is tangled and the frayed tatters of the landscape whistle past. One of the windows cracks, the car is like a knife slicing through the darkness. Despite the speed, I begin to make out figures by the roadside, familiar faces. What is this road on which I am traveling? What two places does it connect? Over what ground does it run? Some of the people are riding donkeys, others are on foot. I see Marx and Engels standing in a traffic booth. I see Rosa Luxemburg with a China rose in her hair, with her hand out, hitching a lift. Lenin is pushing a wheelbarrow filled with hardened cement, as though he had been about to build something but ran out of the time, and the cement dried out. I see Che Guevara, his beard sparse, trudging silently, wheeling his punctured bicycle.

I want to overtake this long line of people, but the speed of the car and of the dream will not let me. Nor will the driver. There is a struggle, I want to leave my people far behind, but the car continues to crawl along, and in the rear-view mirror, I see them staring at me, stoic, imperturbable, their faces saying: Save us, comrade. Take us with you, comrade. And then the nightmare becomes disturbing.

I do not want to, but I arrive at the future alone. The car stops, I get out, the car rounds a bend and disappears. The black figure of the driver does not explain. And yet I know that he has more important things to do now. In the future, there is nothing. This is the most pleasant moment of the nightmare. It is not troubling that there is nothing. I discover this now, at the eleventh hour, and I wait to see what happens. And this is the tale told to me by the future, a respectable, garrulous gentleman.

A European tourist has arrived at my hotel, it is his first day. Sitting in the lobby, he smokes a cigarette, watching the whorls of smoke. On his head, he is wearing a black bowler hat. A sweater, also black, with the white question mark over the breast, and over this, a suit – the jacket and pants in a mustard-and-gray striped fabric. Very elegant, our tourist. On his face, drawn in pencil, a faint smile is about to break. The tourist is reading a magazine he brought from Europe, with a special supplement about our country that explains our customs – without stereo-typing, that goes without saying. A double-page spread tells the story of a prostitute. The tourist looks at the photograph. He finds her beautiful, a little battered by fate, but attractive nonetheless.

It is an unspecified day of an unspecified year of an unspecified decade. The tourist walks out of the hotel, heads up the avenue and stops three streets later, on a crowded corner, outside a cinema with no films scheduled. From among the crowd, as though put there by the hand of God, emerges a slim, very sensual figure. A woman with chestnut hair, svelte, tender eyes, high cheekbones. Ample hips. Ample buttocks.

The woman asks for a cigarette. The tourist gives her one. The woman asks what he is smiling at. At nothing says the tourist, this is how his face is. She says something like, What a strange face. The tourist touches his lips, tries to form an expression of wonder, but it immediately turns into an expression of happiness. You're the woman in the magazine, the tourist says. The woman, who is now smoking, does not know what the tourist is talking about and looks at him in surprise. A little shamefaced, he takes the magazine from his pocket, finds the article. The woman takes the magazine, glances at it, recognizes herself and confirms, yes, that's her. Then the woman reads the article, not out of curiosity, since she knows her own life by heart, but for the pleasure of seeing herself acknowledged, a little alien to herself. The tourist invites her for a drink, and they walk off and end up in an isolated, unrecognizable café. They sit on plastic seats at a small table.

The woman elaborates on her story, and the tourist listens to her, spellbound. The woman says that, some months ago, one night, she was on a train. She was traveling from a city to the country, to the place where she was born and where her son still lives in the care of her neighbors. It had been months, many months, since she last saw him and she was bringing him presents. Clothes, toys, the woman says, and a little money, you know. The woman speaks in short sentences, but not without self-assurance. She pauses, is silent, then takes a deep breath. It seems as though she does not want to carry on. The tourist is giving her his full attention. The woman has already drunk a beer. The tourist asks if she would like another, the woman nods. Another round, the tourist calls. He glances around and realizes that he does not know where he is. The woman carries on with her story. A man comes up to her on the train, he has a foreign accent, but she never suspected that the man was a journalist, nor that he would want to tell her story anywhere. Besides, we are in the future, and the woman does not really care that someone has revealed intimate details of her life in a magazine in a country that is not her own.

The tourist is seized by the conviction that the woman is very beautiful, and also the conviction that he will not tell her so. He is struck by a feeling of foreboding: he will not be able to touch her. If he touches her, he will feel as though he is sullying or corrupting her, although the tourist has not believed in such things for a long time, nor does he approach the world through genteel words and prudishness. It is therefore ridiculous to think that a prostitute could still retain a certain purity, something worthy of saving, something that other men have not trampled, brutalized and used without a flicker of remorse or even a fleeting bitterness.

The man on the train, the woman tells the tourist, sat in one of those darkened carriages on trains and I thought he was going to offer me a deal. But no. He simply took some photos and asked her some questions. Sometimes in shadow, sometimes in the light. Almost always in the shadows, but from time to time, as they were passing a one-horse country town or a remote sugar refinery, the light revealed his face, the face of a listener. I asked myself questions too, the woman says, but silently, to myself. What is this foreigner doing on a provincial train? More than that. What is he doing on a local train in the middle of the night? More than that. What is he doing on a local train, in the middle of the night, talking to me, when we could just fuck and get it over with? The woman then goes on to explain how, on the train, she related to the journalist the vicissitudes, the difficulties and the pressures that had led her to take this path. The prostitute was a university student. She had studied chemical engineering, but then the 'difficult years' came along and swept away her future.

The tourist tries to lighten the atmosphere, though the woman's tone is never somber or upset. That's something I heard from my friends, the tourist says, in this country, prostitutes are university students, they are beautiful and very wholesome. The woman does not smile, she does nothing. She looks at him just as she would have if he had kept his mouth shut. The atmosphere becomes tense and one, two, three, a procession of clouds scud across the sky of the future. How can your problem be solved? the tourist asks the woman, and the woman, after taking a breath, but without hesitating over her answer, says: with a hundred dollars, darling, every problem can be solved with a hundred dollars. I'd like to give you the money as a gift, says the tourist. You can't gift it to me, says the woman, I'm a professional.

For several minutes they argue until, by mutual agreement, they decide to go to the nightclub in the hotel where the tourist is staying, which is my hotel. They gesticulate, speaking in low voices. The tourist is keen to walk, the woman wants to take a taxi. In the end, they seem to embrace, or to reconcile, and they set off on foot. They cross a number of streets, pass various crumbling buildings, far from the tourist sector, past building sites, condemned houses, decaying mansions with railings covered in rust and gates with metal door knockers. A dog barks but they carry on walking and eventually distance and darkness swallow up the barking.

They arrive at the nightclub, in the basement of the hotel. They avoid the dance floor and sit at a table for two very close to the bar. All the while, the tourist has been insisting that the woman take the money and she has refused, which means that the atmosphere has become uncomfortable and neither now has much desire to sleep with the other, although the tourist has known from the start that he cannot sleep with this woman.

Go on, he says, take the money. Silence. It's a gift, go on, take it. Silence. Then a waitress appears, who turns out to be my daughter María, even more beautiful than the prostitute, and she asks what they would like to drink. They order a margarita and a gin and tonic. The noise, the deafening music, my daughter coming over with the drinks. It is obvious that something is about to happen. My daughter sets the drinks down on the table. The tourist takes out a hundred-dollar bill, shows it to the prostitute, makes sure she is watching, and gives it to my daughter as a tip.

The music begins to become clearer. A song that, casually listened to, says nothing that one might want to hear and that, carefully listened to, says nothing either. A song that has little to say and is barely worth dancing to. But the woman and the tourist are not dancing. They are

71

wary not to utter a word or a sound. Suddenly, my daughter comes back, strobed by the lights of the dance floor, and says that she cannot accept the tip, that it is too much money and she is not allowed to accept it. My daughter watches as the tourist's face changes, the worried eyes, the wrinkled brow. The woman, on the other hand, sees something very different: a faint smile, drawn in pencil, but one that, to all appearances, looks as though it cannot possibly crack or fade or disappear.

Instantly, having reappeared, the black car and the dark figure of the driver come and pick me up. I get into the car and make the journey back, back to the morning and the real world. I see Che Guevara with his punctured bicycle, I see Lenin with his wheelbarrow of cement, I see Rosa Luxemburg with the China rose in her hair, I see Marx and Engels in the traffic booth. The pain of it! All these brilliant minds leaving just as I arrive. That is the nightmare, that is the future.

The Daughter

He looks as though a blast wave consumed the right side of his body, as though an alien creature has taken a bite out of him, I swear.

At twelve, René was still living in Oriente, in a strange town called Moa which means The Desolate Place, or The Place of the Dead, a truly bizarre place. In Occidente, we'd never even heard of it. René says it's a city of considerable resources that could be prosperous if only its inhabitants got a percentage of the profits. But it's in Oriente and, in eastern Cuba, people are poorer than anywhere else, they *have* to be, it's practically the law. The Desolate Place or The Place of the Dead was hardly likely to be an exception, especially with a name like that.

René was brought up by his neighbors as his mother had to leave when he was very young. The 'difficult years' had made things impossible and the boy was likely to starve to death or grow up deformed. His mother headed west to Occidente to earn a living. René never knew why his mother had abandoned him, until one day he found out – things always come out in the end.

Their neighbors didn't approve of the mother, they didn't like the fact she prostituted herself. René heard the rumors but they were no more than insinuations, a secret language or message he had to decode and which, in the end, obviously, he managed to decode. And although they helped him in other ways, what the neighbors really wanted was for René to crack the code, for the bomb to explode. Rumors are the fuel that keep small towns alive.

René locked himself in his room, buried his head in the pillow, but didn't cry. When I asked him about it, on the day he decided to tell me, he said that at the age of twelve he didn't understand the importance of a mother,

that what had scared him was that he didn't think badly of
her, that he didn't think she had failed him or anything,
even though in a way people were encouraging him to
think badly of her. After a while, I don't know how long,
René decided to stop brooding about it and to support his
mother at all costs, and this is what forced him to quickly
become a man. At thirteen, René was stronger than ever,
at fourteen, stronger than he was at thirteen, at fifteen
stronger than at fourteen, and so on.

He dropped out of school, started stealing, developed a
sixth sense for details. He had an eagle eye, that sees little,
but remembers everything it sees. He made skeleton keys,
copper keys that opened every door in the town, and no-
one ever caught him. The Desolate Place or The Place of
the Dead was the largest industrial complex in the country, comprising forty per cent of global reserves in nickel
and twenty-six per cent of cobalt, he told me. The factories were some distance outside the town and there was
never any noise from them. The streets of the Desolate
Place or Place of the Dead were deserted. Everything was
spattered with a red mud, the result of high mineral de-
posits in the soil. The houses, the pavements, the faces of
the people. I told him I found it difficult to imagine and
he said something I liked: he said it was as if the hottest
point of the sun had been ground into powder and settled
over the place.

By sixteen, stronger than he was at fifteen, René had
stolen a lot and was starting to wonder whether he wanted to carry on. As though he had suddenly developed
a conscience. People were already having to deal with
various demons. Health conditions among the workers
and residents of the Desolate Place or Place of the Dead
were appalling. They were suffering the environmental
consequences of the mining operations. There were no

official figures, he told me, but just as rumors grew that his mother was a prostitute, so worse fears now began to grow. Elevated incidences of cancer, respiratory problems, contaminated water, possible chemical radiation. A sickly child was born whom the people of the Desolate Place or Place of the Dead dubbed Pinto Boy, since he had a mole, a gigantic birthmark like a benign tumor that might become malignant. This was enough for René. At seventeen, he gave up his criminal activities and headed off to work at the factories.

Factory One was a mixed processing plant owned by the government and a foreign company. It had acid pressure leaching, considered state-of-the-art technology in nickel extraction. The plant was one of the most efficient in the world. There were piles of waste, paths that glowed orange as though toxic. Trucks carted away soil laden with minerals, fifty tons a load. René saw all this with his eagle eye, he told me.

They sent him to Factory Two, a cavernous, half-ruined city of metal with internal bus routes, its own electrical plant and thunderous, well-oiled machines. The smelting plant was criss-crossed by rivers of leachate, slag runoff like litmus. René showed me some photos; they were disgusting. The ammonia and all the other chemicals made it hard to breathe. Every time he inhaled, he felt his nostrils burning, and thought he might pass out. The other workers breathed normally; they were used to it.

After a few weeks' training, René became a sampler, someone who checked the rotary kilns in which the nickel was processed. He began to live in dark, narrow ducts filled with clouds of burning black dust where the ambient temperature was at the limit of what is bearable. All day, he had a metallic taste in his mouth, on his tongue and his lips. Over time, he told me, the intolerable rumbling of machines became silence. The furnaces became a refuge. He didn't miss stealing, he didn't miss the neighbors, he didn't miss his mother.

At eighteen, René wore tight-fitting overalls, synthetic gloves, a yellow plastic hard hat, a facepiece respirator, and a belt from which hung nozzles and sample bottles. He never said so, but I pictured him like one of those species that live in the depths of the ocean, those blind creatures that no-one has discovered yet. One afternoon, he tripped or fainted – he isn't sure which. He fell against the furnace wall, and the furnace burned part of the right side of his body, fried it. He lost consciousness, obviously. An older woman, also a sampler, stumbled on his body some minutes later. She screamed, they say. But who was there to hear her? No-one . The woman dragged René's body through the narrow duct, climbed a metal staircase and reached the first floor. Here, where there was a little more light, she realized that the furnace had left René disfigured and that the shock would probably kill him.

The shock didn't kill him. René spent six months in hospital and came out alive, although, as anyone can see, he was left with a section of skin that is no more than a giant scar. Part of his right earlobe had to be removed when it became infected. His right arm, right shoulder and right cheek were burned. And there are others, parts that are hidden by his clothes. The range of his vision was reduced, but his eagle eye was intact, he told me, and that is what mattered to René.

His mother told him that everything was fine now and sent for him. René moved to Occidente and arrived in the pueblo. His mother lived there and no longer worked as a prostitute – she had a house and a job with a clandestine company. René started out as a blacksmith's assistant, later he sold feed for horses, even later he got a job at the beach collecting trash. René started work before dawn. He cannot be exposed to the sun for too long. One day, his skin started growing over some of the disfigured parts, and when it had been growing for some time, René realized that there is no more body for the skin to cover, that he has more skin than anything else, more skin than he needs, that it is building up between his fingers. On his right hand, René looked as though he was wearing a glove. He didn't like it, so he had surgery. They cut away all the skin and threw it into the trash.

René went back to work. Things with his mother were going well. She took care of him, determined to make up for lost time, pulled a few strings. René didn't get involved, didn't want to get involved. His eagle eye, he told me, knew where not to look. He started to work at the hotel, he was the new driver, and this is how I met him, when he drove up one day as I was walking to the bus stop. He asked me if I live in the pueblo. I said yes, and, without getting out of the car, he asked me if I wanted to ride with him. I hesitated, but he insisted and I accepted. You've got no chance, I thought. But René was not looking for a chance, he was looking for company and conversation. He said that he had seen me in the hotel, in the staff canteen at lunchtime. He said he thought we had things in common. Really? I say. What things? I say. He couldn't explain and looked very ashamed. He put his hands on the wheel and stared at the road. I couldn't stop thinking about all that burnt, scarred flesh.

Don't worry, I said, I'm sure we've got things in common. René smiled. We didn't say much else. He dropped me off outside my building and I thanked him. I climbed the stairs to the apartment, still thinking we had nothing in common, but that night his repulsive image, this ugly guy, this broken thing, went round and round in my head.

The following day, when I got to the hotel, I went looking for him and said hello. We arranged to have lunch together. It became a habit. We started to fall in love, this was the moment for me to act. I needed a right-hand man at work. I explained to René how the scam worked. He had been there nearly three months and no-one had told him. But he knew something was going on. His eagle eye was powerful. He could read a car license plate from two blocks away.

We didn't traffic meat, drugs or tobacco. Everything we stole, we stole simply so we could live in a minimum of comfort, not to get rich, because here anything that involves getting rich ends in catastrophe. OK, René said, I get it, we live in a country so small that there will come a day when it's not even big enough to house the owner. Sure, however you want to look at it, I said, it is what it is. We stole ham, cheese, bottles of wine, rum, whisky, tins of tuna and sardines, jars of pickles.

Since it is an all-inclusive resort hotel, the amount of food the tourists will consume is carefully calculated in adavance. A figure that is invariably inflated. The excess is divvied up between the works and the security guards. The maintenance staff and the drivers are the only people authorized to move between the various parts of the hotel. The contraband is transported from place to place in their bags, their toolboxes, their briefcases. Sometimes, at the last minute, word goes round and the whole thing has to be nixed. There's an inspection scheduled, and we can't risk it. It's funny, in a way, because the guest's account has already been settled, the goods have already been signed off, and it would be suspicious if there was a surplus. So we have to make it disappear. We slice the ham and the cheeses, use bandages and surgical tape to stick it to our bellies, our backs, our legs, and smuggle it out that way.

Despite everything, business was brisk. There was enough food to bring home and even to sell a little. I made enough to buy Mamá an automatic washing machine, and I started thinking about redecorating the apartment. René started siphoning off some of the petrol allocated to the hotel. He stole it and I found people to buy it. One way or another, I felt like things were taking off, until my father was appointed manager of the hotel. In his first week, he fired five people, and even thought about laying me off. Not because he caught me doing anything, but because I'm his daughter and the very thought of nepotism gets him riled up. He tried to fire me but can't.

My father decided that, of all the chauffeurs working at the hotel, René should be his driver. I didn't like the idea, and René found it worrying. But we couldn't object, we just bided our time. I went round to René's house at night and talked to his mother. I observed their relationship. When Mamá started to get sick, I felt completely devastated. I didn't feel like doing anything, but I had to carry on stealing. René supported me and I got used to his physical abnormalities. I started to see anyone who hasn't suffered burns down their right side as deformed.

René gave me a slightly bigger percentage of the profits from the his sale of siphoned gas. Mamá took to him, as did my father, though for very different reasons. René was generous to me and to Mamá, and with my father he was respectful and disciplined. With his own mother, he was kind of intense. I knew she hadn't been a good mother, the way mine was. But it didn't matter now they were together and happy. I thought about this one day when I saw them hugging, or another time when I saw them joking around and arguing. They argued, they fought, they patched things up, and no-one was traumatized by any of it. There were no falls, no dramas.

It seems stupid now, but in the moment, that's not how I felt. I realized that I no longer had a healthy mother with whom I could do things like this. All her years of being a perfect mother no longer matter, they've melted away. These days, even an ex-prostitute is more of a mother than she is. I stopped going round to René's house. We carried on with the business, but René started getting careless and stealing more than he should. I saw it coming, but I didn't say anything. Then my father discovered forty liters of petrol allocated to his Nissan had gone missing. He found out where René stashed the fuel, and fired him on the spot.

René tried to explain but my father wouldn't let him. So he came to ask me to intervene. I can't get involved right now, I said. René feels that I betrayed him. No-one else believes that – René getting fired has seriously affected me financially. I know, René said. But you ratted me out, he said. How do you know? I said. I know, he said, then turned on his heel and walked away, with his eagle eye and his charred flaccid skin.

I haven't seen him since. But that doesn't surprise me; nothing surprises me. The only thing that surprises me – go figure – is that if you don't think about it, you don't notice. But if you do think about it, even for a second, there's always some tiny part of your body that is about to itch or ache.

IV

The Son

I have ten days left before I'm discharged. I'll finally get out of this dump and be able to go to university, far from this shithole of a pueblo. The other recruits have been congratulating me, they wish they were in my shoes. But they never studied, never did anything, and you can't go through life like that and expect it to throw you a bone. They're all my age, more or less, and they think they still have a chance because that's what they've been told, when self-evidently they have none. For a man, the margin between being drowned and saved is a narrow one, and usually occurs at an age – fourteen, maybe fifteen – when he is unaware of it, has no idea what is at stake, which explains why humanity is little more than an endless parade of the disappointed, of bastards being led to the stocks, living through day after day for no particular reason, watching in disbelief as their experience, I think, is no different to that of the rest of the species – growth and maturity, minor aches, major traumas, the gradual loss of physical faculties, gray hair and wrinkles, lameness, deafness, and ultimately decay and disgust.

By eighteen, nineteen, twenty, a man is already irrevocably what he is, his path has already been traced and he can do nothing to change it. It would be healthier if everyone optimized their lives based on the role assigned to them rather than spending time trying to transform themselves into something they can never become. I'm not saying it's fair, but that's how it is. The absurdity of life is not that it comes to an end. That it ends is, actually, less absurd than the preposterousness of it beginning. The absurdity of life is its uneven distribution, I think, the manifest internal imbalance of episodes, the uneven distribution of major events. Before the age of twenty, a transcendental maelstrom is continually bubbling, a stew that never ceases to reverberate, and we cannot digest everything that life serves up to us. There are constantly new signs to interpret, signals and feints flashing past, third and fourth dimensions. At twenty, at precisely twenty, everything is in place.

After that, I think, comes a stretch of barren years: the thirties, the forties, the fifties, the sixties. Then, supposedly, man acquires wisdom. I can't comment, since I haven't reached that point, but I can't help but wonder what purpose wisdom serves a man if all that he can do with it is look back on the things he didn't do before he had that wisdom, and torment himself with all the things he might have done if he'd had it. In the end, the whole thing is a waste, if not of time, then of incidents which, before twenty, come so thick and fast it's impossible to truly experience them. Honestly, a thousand things have happened to me that I did not truly experience.

Right now, I'm sitting on the edge of my cot bed, I've just masturbated in the latrine fantasizing about damp underwear, a damp stain of urine, genitals constantly dripping. I am lacing up my boots, preparing for the 8.00 p.m. guard duty, an easy shift, one of my last in this shithole, when another soldier comes up to me, a skinny guy, a raw recruit whose name I don't know, one who is forever asking stupid questions, probably just to shock, but I don't like being asked questions, or being idolized, I have no desire to mentor or to take pupils under my wing the way so many strapping old soldiers did and still do with soldiers who are scrawny or new. Even so the skinny guy says, hey, Diego, is it true what Solano has been saying? And I ask what's Solano been saying, and he tells me what Solano told him, that I've been disguising my voice and phoning my mother to insult her. I don't lose

my cool, naturally, I carry on doing up my boots, threading the lace through one eyelet then the next, zigzagging
like a lizard, and, without looking up, I ask the skinny
guy when Solano said this, and the skinny guy says just
now, and I ask him if Solano is on Sentry Post Two, and
the skinny guy says yes, and then he asks me whether it's
true or not, and I say no, it's not true, I want to call him
by name but I don't know it, of course it's not true, I say,
and the skinny guy asks if it's serious, my mother's illness. Everyone in the unit knows my mother is ill, and
I tell him I don't know, I finish threading the lace, pull it
tight, get to my feet, readjust my uniform pants, ask the
skinny guy again if he's sure about what Solano said and
the skinny guy says, yeah, Diego, I'm sure, he says you
call her in the middle of the night and sometimes during
the day and you put on a fake voice.

The skinny guy cannot gauge the magnitude of what
he is saying because he hasn't been here long. When I
was like he is now, a raw recruit, Solano showed up an
hour late to relieve me from a sentry shift. Solano is
twenty now, he joined the unit before I did, but I'll be
leaving before him. When he got back, I was waiting
for him back in the dorm. I knew the drill. He was going
to brazen it out, try to convince me it was an induction
ritual and, if I gave in, he would carry on taking advant-
age of me along with the rest of the older recruits. My
shifts would get longer. I didn't give him time to speak, I
grabbed my *zambrán* and lashed out, brutally driving the
buckle into his back. He was winded. His body creaked
and he let out a snort, like a castrated animal. He doubled
over, but I didn't let up. I kicked him in the face and broke
his nose. Then I whipped him across the back again. His
skin instantly rose in two vicious welts. I thought about
the hour this fuckwit had left me at my post just because

he thought it was funny, and I felt blind rage sweep over me again. Even so, I didn't carry on, there was no need.

I spent several weeks waiting for a revenge attack that never came. I realized that Solano was a coward and that my brutal beating did me no credit, but I wasn't looking for credit. I'd just wanted it to be effective, and it had been: no-one dared mess with me, the relief guard turned up on time and Solano decided to stay out of my way. I had the opportunity to abuse him, crush him, destroy him, but I don't do bullying, so I left him to stew and be eaten up by fear. This gesture of magnanimity simply reinforced the respect that the beating had earned me, but eventually time and routine destroy or desecrate everything, you let down your guard, and after a few weeks I was just another squaddie, subject to the same jokes as everyone else. It didn't bother me, I didn't need to control things, all I wanted was for no-one to have control over me.

Little by little, as these things happen, Solano started to creep closer, at first joining in group conversations, then asking me the occasional question, later chatting to me normally, until finally he was completely reinstated. From time to time, someone would mention the beating I'd given him, and I would intervene to defuse the comment. I didn't want the relationship to go off the rails again. I was just trying to survive, to get a bit of peace in this military cesspit, hoping against hope that the war really would not come, because I didn't believe in the war, just as I don't believe in it now, but it was mentioned so often, announced so often, that I began to have doubts. I remember I came back from leave without a flicker of humor in my body after the debacle with Armando, I got through my day on duty, twelve whole hours, and the next day off was one of the worst because they shipped us off in a truck to a quarry on the outskirts of the town, on the way to the beach, to gather quicklime, we were to fill a couple of fifty-five gallon polyethylene tanks and, when we got back, we were supposed to whitewash the walls of the barracks.

After two hours in the quarry, I lay down on a couple of cardboard boxes in the shade of the truck. I couldn't sleep, because the rest of the soldiers moved closer in and the constant drone of conversation was impossible to block out completely, and so I floated in the shallows of consciousness, not very deep, about a foot below the surface. Then I felt a freezing jet that made my heart stop, a cold, viscid, burning substance, and instantly I knew it was quicklime, there was nothing else it could be. I scrabbled to my feet, the soldiers were laughing, they were all laughing and joking, but I wasn't laughing and joking, I was furious and serious, and now the quicklime was trickling down my chest, soaking my shirt, and there was Solano. He didn't look as though he had done it maliciously, and even at the time I didn't think he was the confrontational type, but he'd encroached on my interests again and I had to teach him a lesson. It must have been obvious from my face, because the atmosphere was suddenly tense. The laughter gave way to silence, and someone said, just leave it, Diego, but I strode over to Solano, gripping my *zambrán* belt, and he stood stock-still, a flicker of defiance in his eyes, a faint glimmer none of the other soldiers could see. But I could see it, and, to be honest, I didn't want to fight, but I knew that if I lashed out, I'd have to fight, Solano looked like he was about to say something. What if I toss you into that hole? I said nodding to the pool of quicklime a few meters away. What about that? He didn't say anything. I could still see the glimmer, but he didn't say anything, and in the end that was enough for me, for him to say nothing, for the soldiers to think that I could have tossed him into the quicklime, that I was capable of and prepared to do it and that, if I wanted it, that was the most likely outcome. But I wasn't so sure that I could do such a thing and I didn't want to risk it: I saw something in Solano that I did not like one bit, and I stopped threatening him. I'm not going to do it, I said. I grabbed him by the collar and gave him a gentle little headbutt, one that was friendly and aggressive at the same time.

We haven't spoken since then, haven't exchanged a single world, and now this skinny guy comes and tells me what Solano has been saying. I buckle my *zambrán,* leave the dormitory and head to Sentry Post Two, I see him in the courtyard, sitting on a stool, chatting to a bunch of other soldiers, this is the time of day when no-one sleeps. I walk over and confront him, ask him what he's been saying, and Solano, who's learned his lesson, does not reply, lands a vicious punch to my nose and I feel an electric shock spread across my face, I hurl myself at him and we both go sprawling, I can't see a thing, we roll on the grass, twisting and struggling, me in my *zambrán*, my boots and my uniform, he in his *zambrán*, boots and uniform, we are not doing each other much damage and we know it, we stop throwing futile punches, we are too close, too entangled for our punches to complete their trajectory and inflict damage, quite the opposite, we are a writhing mass of snorts and insults, I call him a mother-fucker and he calls me a faggot, I try to bite him, he tries to do something with his elbow to my back, I don't know what, sometimes I'm on top, sometimes he is, none of the soldiers get involved, the sentry on duty doesn't intervene, a real man wouldn't do what you've done, Solano says, you're a sick faggot, he says, you're an arse bandit, he says, I heard you, he says, I heard you, you faggot, I don't say anything, our energy quickly burns out, I can feel the fatigue in my muscles and I know that Solano must feel it too. It's at this point that the fight becomes aware of itself, realizes it cannot draw on resources better suited to a different form of confrontation, one where there is space between the adversaries, rather than the tangle of limbs to which all these months spent as soldiers waiting for war has reduced us, and so we shift to street fighting, battling over every sector of our bodies, a small-scale war in which close-combat weapons, the fingers and the mouth, take on a fundamental role, I stare into his eyes and he stares into mine, but his hand finds my mouth and tugs at the corner of my lips, I manage to sink my teeth into his index finger, but fail to latch on tightly and he jerks his hand away. Even so, he howls. Then his hand scrabbles for my eyes, tries to gouge them out, and it feels as though he just might succeed, I am completely shattered and he's still screaming faggot, and what he's saying no longer riles or angers me, it simply makes me sink deeper, I feel a wave of real fear and this makes me go limp, Solano is gripping me, I feel as though I am floating, drifting away, but I'd rather he punch me than gouge an eye out, anything but that, and then, thank god, the duty sentry finally shows up, pulls us apart and saves me.

This is what I am thinking as I scrabble to my feet, my nose gushing blood. You've got ten days, Diego, then you're out of here. Nothing matters. You managed to fool them all and come through this whole thing unscathed. Ten days and you're gone. But I don't have ten days left. The duty sentry will report this incident to the lieutenant colonel in charge of the unit, who will defer my discharge by three weeks, through which I'll practically float. During this enforced extension, I am made of helium. I am a noble gas, and meanwhile the other soldiers no longer show up on time to relieve me. I end up doing five-hour sentry shifts, but I don't protest, I don't say a word. The punch-up was so absurd, a lightning flash I cannot get my head around. I know I'm the victim of a conspiracy. The skinny guy gives me looks of pity and disgust, the sort of look you might give to cynics or to vanquished powers.

The Mother

We were in the shower, Armando was scrubbing my back. I can't shower by myself. The loofah was scraping the brittle film of my skin. Armando had been home for four hours, but I still hadn't said a word.

He carried on telling me what had happened with the same slowness as the events he was recounting. He went into his office and ushered them in. One by one they sat down, still cordial. There were three, four, maybe five of them. No-one knows how many officious little men there are. Armando asked his secretary to bring coffee. The sponge continued to move down my back like a rolling pin. They took their cups and sipped slowly, painstakingly. Then one of them asked after me, how has your wife been, he said. Armando said that we hadn't given up hope and that we were still working towards some improvement. It's the only way, another said. Everyone needs to do their bit. Some people take their own lives, the depression, the pessimism, they said. It's a scientific fact, another said, you have to have a positive mental attitude, always stay optimistic.

One of them noticed that this was not a particularly congenial topic and changed the subject. Armando still didn't really understand what this was all about. The sponge swabbed my armpits, my neck, beneath my sagging breasts, more gently now. They talked without really getting to the point, about the three classification models used to categorize hotel establishments. The presence/absence system that requires certain essential services for a hotel in each category. Armando's hotel was categorized as a four-star, and lacked a number of inclusive amenities which meant that, however hard he worked, it would be impossible for it to progress to the highest category.

They asked him whether he was happy running a four-star hotel or whether he would like to manage a five-star property. Armando said that he was a soldier and that it was not a matter of what he wanted, but what was asked of him, where he could be most useful. If his next hotel was a five-star property, all well and good. If it was a three-star, it made no difference. The officious little men exchanged sly looks. One of them shifted his feet, settled himself in his chair and cleared his throat. He seemed to be the leader of the delegation. The soap slipped off the handle of the shower door and skittishly landed under the washbasin.

Very good coffee, they said. Armando thanked them as though he were the Food and Beverage Manager or as though the quality of the coffee, more than any other indicator, defined his efficiency and skill as Director. Having finished bathing me, Armando turned off the shower and handed me a towel. Are you going to dry yourself, or would you like me to dry you? he asked. He let me dry myself. We left the bathroom and I got dressed, still half wet. A pair of panties and a light housecoat.

They asked him why he had refused to send two workers on military maneuvers and replace them with the two candidates that the Party Official had humbly proposed. I didn't see any compelling reason to do so, he answered. I was sitting on the bed and Armando was leaning against the door frame of our bedroom, visibly bewildered, as though suddenly a barrowload of years had fallen on his shoulders and the old age he had pictured had swirled down the drain. The officious little men shifted their chairs closer, circling him. One of them, the apparent leader, got to his feet, and began to pace up and down the office.

We believe, Armando, that you colluded with the two workers in question to steal from the hotel. His outline dissolved in the yellow glow of the light from the dining room. I have never stolen anything, he said, how could anyone even think that? We are going to have to replace you, said the officious little man. What reasons did they give you? I asked. We don't want to drag things out, Armando, said the officious little man, it would be best if you were to accept our decision, we will reassign you to a post more in keeping with your capabilities. Let's go into the living room, I said. The heat was killing me, the steam from the bathroom had started to mingle with the vaporous air. He followed unquestioningly, he couldn't even raise his head.

I don't think this is fair, Armando said, opening the top button of his shirt. Don't waste our time, they said to him, we came to talk to you to ensure that you will accept our solution without protest. You have been conspiring with various staff members in this hotel, you have been illicitly skimming funds and you have dismissed everyone who got in the way. Why have you allowed your daughter to continue working in the same hotel? they said. Our daughter was working there before you took over, I said. That is irrelevant, they said, all the staff members you fired were also working here before you took over. Your daughter has made a small fortune from this hotel, and you haven't lifted a finger. I raised my daughter, Armando said, she is incapable of taking something that does not belong to her. Armando told the officious little men the story of Che Guevara and the bicycle factory and insisted that it was by these same principles that he had raised his family.

Perhaps we should believe you, Armando, they said. Perhaps it's true that you knew nothing and had nothing to do with what has been going on in this hotel. What is surprising is that you seem to know less about your own daughter than we do. Armando swallowed hard. I held out my hand and he took it. What do I need to know? he said. You fired your driver, the leader of the officious little men said, and immediately afterwards, for no reason, your Nissan started running out of gas. What did you do with the gas, Armando? Did you fire your driver because, as you claim, he was stealing, or did you fire him so that you could carry on stealing with impunity? We have also discovered that your driver suffers from a physical disability, something you did not take into consideration. He's not disabled, I said. Be that as it may, said the officious little man, but he does have some kind of problem.

I wanted to ask Armando if they were going to fire María too, but I didn't need to. We are not going to dismiss your daughter, said the officious little man, only you are to be officially sanctioned. I breathed more easily. I felt bad for my husband, I felt terribly sorry, but one doesn't cancel out the other. If they fired María, the whole house would fall apart. I ran a hand over my head and my fingers tangled in a lock of hair. Armando sank deeper into his chair. He had taken off his shoes, and his brown socks made him look abandoned and destitute. He had not yet realized it, but he was a man who had begun to turn the other way, like a rope that has been twisted. The officious little men told him they were dismissing him for stealing, but the officious little men had no problem with those who stole.

The truth is, they were firing him because he refused to accept others stealing, but since they couldn't tell him that, they told him they were dismissing him for stealing, an explanation that, even though Armando had never laid a finger on another person's property, his ears were more prepared to accept. In fact, after a time, his mind would manage to persuade him that at some point he must have

unwittingly stolen, without realizing, and thus the pun-
ishment regained its justness.

You will give up your position in a week, said the leader of the officious little men. The delegation got to their
feet and, cordially, one by one, they shook his hand and
said their goodbyes. The empty coffee cups on the office
table. You're ill, Armando said, and now here I am waiting on another job. What's going to happen? There was
obviously no point my telling him. We'll get through this,
I said. We always do, we've been through worse times. He
nodded slowly.

In that moment, I wanted to give him something more,
after so many years of giving him nothing. A sliver of
truth, at least, but not all of it. He sat there in his chair
and I turned on the TV. There was something I couldn't
name. For the first time in my life I was trying to venture
into Armando's world so that I could console him. But it
wasn't like when you forget a word. It's not that. It's not
as though I had the words on the tip of my tongue and
couldn't get them out. And it's not one of those words that
you don't know but instinctively realize exists, that it is
there, in a shop window, just waiting for people to go in
and try it on and say what they need to say and then leave
it where they found it so someone else can come and use
it. What I needed for my husband was not a word that
illuminated a specific meaning, but a word that was, in-
trinsically, its meaning.

I kissed Armando on the lips, cold and dry as an old
peel, and I went back to my bed, my spiritual retreat. I
knew that, as time went on, I knew less and less and that
this yawning gap of obliviousness and impairment would
continue to grow. But each time I knew less, each time
something new refused to let me name it, I also realized
that there was nothing better than not knowing, than not

naming, not speaking, not explaining, not being able to. I
slept peacefully that night, sheltered by the sickness.

The Father

I fix myself a drink. I see a helplessness in Mariana's eyes.
The curious thing about her expressions is that they have
to be deciphered like a code, maybe the marriage code.
No-one but me could understand them. To the untrained
eye, Mariana's expression could be summed up as one of
those looks that tries to say nothing, to conceal what it
is trying to express, or to let the other person know that
whatever the look might be expressing, however true,
has not the least value, and whether or not it is expressed
doesn't even matter. It doesn't bother Mariana that I drink.
She knows it's a habit, but one that I can control. Time
was, when we were young, she would sometimes drink
with me. I still ask, but these days she no longer wants to
join me.

She looks down at her blouse, at the stains it has accumulated in the kitchen, her very own commendations.
Everything, I think, will be fine, it is the most normal
thing in the world. The dialectical wheel of existence rises
and falls, it is seasonal. The flow of tourists does not constantly arrive at target destinations at the same rate. Since
the arrival of tourists is not uniform, but focused on certain months, we say that it is seasonal. High seasons have
peaks and low seasons have troughs, but however acute
the fortunes or misfortunes, we come through them.

You can't drink too much, Mariana says. Just a little more, I say. I am sitting on the wicker sofa with my
feet up. I open my eyes, sigh, press my lips together
and, hesitant to swallow, I move the liquid around my
mouth. Mariana runs her fingers through my hair. Her
hand does not move smoothly, my hair is thick and her
fingers rough. I squeeze her hips and carry on swilling the
drink around my mouth. A little rum mixed with spittle

escapes and trickles down my chin. The liquid trace collects into a droplet and falls onto my pants. Mariana has told me that María never stole anything and I suspect that this is true because, if she had stolen, how could we forgive her? They've been trying to pressure me. I thought that a man was best judged by his position in society, but a man is his family. His wife and children.

I pour myself another drink. There are few chasms as great as that between drinking alone and drinking with someone. When Diego comes home, I'll put my arm around his shoulder, I'll hug him and apologize. He's almost nineteen, and it's time that we started drinking together. He should be here now, but we heard that a few of the other soldiers fell ill and he offered to stay at the barracks for another three weeks. That's not nothing. It's the direct result of the principles we taught him here at home. Make sacrifices, take the first step.

We have a lot of hopes tied up in that boy. We expect him to go a little farther than we did. Because that is the way of things. A surname is not borne in vain, it is borne to remind you where you come from, who put you here, or upon what mountain of bones you are standing. My father was an immigrant from Galicia who arrived in the country early in the century. He settled in Occidente, but in the central region, in the lush prairie. He cut mangroves, made charcoal, sowed rice and managed to buy his little plot of land where he made a living as a horse trader.

The acrid smell that tickled my grandfather's nostrils still lingers. This is a pueblo fecund with the dry bittersweet dust of horseshit, and with the sea a few kilometers away, even if we turn our back on it. The last street in the pueblo, the street that leads to the train station, the street where my grandfather settled, where my father started out in life, where later I started out, is broad but deserted, with much light on the asphalt, with light that trickles down the gutters and light in the potholes, as though light were contained in a glass and the glass had tipped over. No-one comes here. Beyond this street is the sea, the rugged coastline, the reef. The beach and the hotels have stolen the limelight.

But my father knew these places, and it was from here, thanks to my grandfather, that he set out. He became a primary school teacher and later gave classes in various colleges and burnished by the luster of experience, when the time came, he taught up in the mountains, before once more coming came back to the old wooden house. He never truly moved away, yet all these comings and goings, at a time when I did not yet exist and there was no guarantee that I would ever exist, had already begun to make their mark on me. I was already being defined, molded. Man is born old, with a burden on his shoulders. If a man is not destined to be of this earth, then he never was, but if he is to be, then he exists long before he is born.

This is the stock I come from, and I thought it was enough for me that, in me, the family name had reached its apogee, that I was born in the nick of time. All the historical portents suggested as much. The people were marching towards a bright future, along the perfectly paved road of the future, we had only to keep marching, to move from one point to another. But the family name did not end with me: my daughter and son were born, and they took on the burden that I had carried, what until that time had been mine. Now they probably believe that the family name ends with them, and I won't be the one to tell them that it doesn't end with them – I will let them believe, though the truth is that the name does not end with them, no way.

Don't drink any more, Mariana says. Stop now, Armando, you've had enough for today. When you drink alone, alcohol makes you feel like you've got company. And when you drink with others, it makes you feel a little alone. Alcohol tells me that the war will not come now, that it will never come, that I am no longer waiting for it. The future came and went, war never came, and no-one noticed. But a person can't be expected to know everything. In any case, Mariana thinks that I know nothing, but I do know a thing or two. Better yet, I choose what I want to know. The officious little men have had their revenge on me, but this is still an isolated incident and there's nothing to prove otherwise. They want me to take this to another level, but I can't see beyond what's happening to me, and and that's that. The officious little men taking their revenge. What is there to be gleaned from a group of individuals in an office firing another individual? The great cathedrals of philosophy and justice remain standing – they are unaffected by what goes on in offices.

Now that I have some free time, I have been thinking about going back to the last street in the pueblo, wandering around what used to be my home. For months I have been shuttling between the hotel and this apartment which I call home because it was allocated to me, just as this television is my television, this telephone is my telephone because they gave it to me, but what was your home is something no-one can ever take from you. That's what my parents told me. This is your home, *hijo*, you will always have a home here. But I founded a family, and a new family inevitably brings about the destruction of the old. We are a bridge between the people from whom we come and those towards whom we go.

Give me that bottle, Mariana says. Stop sniveling, Armando, stop sniveling. My wife is mad, I'm not sniveling. I am stone cold sober. She is going to die sooner than I thought. I never expected that. Don't die, I say. No, Mariana. Even though we will live on in our children. If a man is not to be of this earth, then he never was, but if ever he once was, then he will always be.

The Daughter

Grandmother's house was a wooden house on the out-skirts of the pueblo, near the sea. Through the chinks between the slats of the wall, sunlight slashed the living room and the bedrooms, as though slicing them into two or three. I remember some gray sparrows used to nest in the rafters under the roof. In the kitchen, there were two tall, narrow windows with railings. There was a table in one corner and two battered leather armchairs. There was a dresser where all the plates and glasses were stored when they had been washed. The glasses always faced down. And there was always a lady in the house.

My parents worked most of the time. The elderly lady worked too, but in the house. She scraped away the black soot the kerosene stove caked onto the pots and pans. She brewed coffee, even when there was no-one home – they would soon come. Sometimes she sliced bitter oranges, and in my half-crazed childish head, I thought the old lady was chopping the same sun that sliced through chinks and crevices in the walls and left sunbeams hanging in the air, teeming with dust motes. I longed to touch them, but I never could.

Later, someone told me that this lady was my grandmother. In the back yard, she washed linen shirts, polyester skirts, and then hung them on a line strung between two wooden stakes. Above the laundry, to the south, rose the rooftops of the houses, the steeple of the church and a column of smoke that seemed blacker with every passing day.

There was a bitter orange tree and an old cherry tree. A cherry tree in such heat is a curious thing, no? It produced small green fruits, almost always bitter, that I would greedily chew until my tortured little girl's lips shriveled and refused to chew any more. That wizened tree beneath the blazing sun was a pitiful sight, to be honest. Even when I was very little I didn't like to see such things, and so I decided not to battle against things that could not be fixed.

Later, my brother was born, though at the time I didn't realize that there could be more members of our family, or that there had been previous members, like my grandmother's husband, a schoolmaster. A little brother hijacks your parents and makes you seek refuge in your grandparents. My mother's parents had also died. So it was my grandmother who took me to school every day and waited at the gate every afternoon when I got out. Then, one day, we moved to the apartment. It was like a machine that my parents had set in motion without telling anyone. Grandmother carried on picking me up from school and taking care of Diego during the day until Mamá got home from work.

She died when I was ten and Diego five. I knew even before my parents said anything. At ten, you notice everything, respond to everything, but say nothing. You say nothing but stow the information away for future use. You're protected by your age, it's like a cloak of invisibility. People see you, but they still think you're not there, that you're not watching when you look, not listening when you hear, not understanding when you do.

I not only saw my grandmother's death coming, I saw how my mother went looking for food when my father went looking for nothing, and how Mamá would open her arms and my father would say: I can't, I can't. I saw the cruel hand of the 'difficult years' squeeze our throats, and no-one saw that I could see, just as no-one saw that my brother was starting to see except me. And I said to him: You can see it now, can't you? He would have been seven, maybe eight. My brother is one of those who learned to see early. And he said: Yes, I see it. Though knee-high to grasshoppers, we could see everything that was going on up there, in the adult world.

We also had the ability to see each other. We were not yet completely invisible. My brother was an eye that watched over me. Mamá would turn out the light at bedtime and in the darkness of the bedroom our bodies would gradually take shape. I would see my brother appear out of the black hole of the night, his wide eyes like glowing embers that refuse to be engulfed. He was five years younger than I was, but I was already beginning to respect him.

And there I am, one afternoon, sitting on the toilet. My growing breasts, two sharp points, and, I don't know how, my brother is there with me, staring at me and smiling. My knickers are pooled around my ankles. I release a yellow jet, a golden stream that falls into the stagnant water, and I feel the flow slow to a trickle. I want to keep on urinating but I can't. My brother says: Why do you pee like that, María? I want to tell him to go away but I don't say it. I've got an invisible finger, I say, a finger that lifts up and presses down and cuts off my pee. So are you playing with your finger? my brother asks. Yes, that's right, I'm playing with my finger, I say. I don't know why I'm talking to him like this. Why am I mimicking the language of our parents, when I know that my brother can see and that we shouldn't talk to each other like this.

He carries on staring, with his short, fearful stature. Is it a magic finger? he asks finally. I can't see it. Yes, it's magic. Oh, OK, he says. I pull up my knickers without wiping myself. Then we carry on growing up, each accumulating more years, but now my brother is older than me. There always comes a day when your little brother overtakes you, flashing past like an arrow. He leaves home, graduates from secondary school, starts military service, abandons the family. So I go to visit him and I say: Listen to me, Mamá isn't well, she's been diagnosed with epilepsy. He decides to come home on one of his leave days and we are delighted. I don't say very much, but I know how to pretend and I go with the flow. We haven't been like this with each other for years, we all behaved well.

We eat and then we pretend to argue because no-one wants to do the dishes. Mamá says: I'm ill. My brother says: I'm going back to the unit in the morning. My father says: I have a lot of work to do. Really? Mamá says. We all laugh. OK, I'll do the dishes, I say. Not just yet, my brother says. I stay and we carry on talking. The evening is going well. About half an hour later, my brother says that he has a story to tell me. And he tells it. This is the moment when he grows smaller, sheds several years and once again becomes younger than me. He still believes that he is old, but he's not. I see how my brother doesn't understand anything, how he has recently regressed to being a little boy with no common sense.

At first, I'm frightened, and then I start to feel happy. This is not in my nature: I don't wish anyone harm, I don't wish my brother harm. I don't know why it's happening to me. I don't say a word, I never say a word. When I can't keep something inside, more often than not, I laugh. My brother thinks I'm laughing at him. What a shame. You reach the sky so soon that you go blind and plummet back to earth.

It happened during the 'Special Period', he says. The town drunk uses the public phone in the local bodega he says, and calls in to a radio show. The empty plates, the cutlery, the half-filled glasses on the table, the wobbly table. It's one of those typical late-night phone-ins you get in every small town in the country. The radio station is one of those local radio stations where everyone knows everyone, the listeners, the presenters, the sound engineers. Everyone knows who is talking to who, knows which leg they limp with, their dreams and their fears.

I'm listening, the disc jockey says to the drunk. I want to request a song, the drunk says. The presenter plays along. From their reaction, I think my parents already know the story. Alright, says the presenter, tell me which song you'd like me to play. But first, I'd like to dedicate it to somebody, the drunk says. That's fine, the presenter says. To a lady friend, perhaps? the presenter says in his affected accent. No, no, not a girlfriend, the drunk says sharply. To who, then? the presenter asks. I'd like to dedicate a song to our comrades in the Communist Party. Even better, the presenter says. And our loyal comrades in government, says the drunk. Excellent, says the presenter. And the police authorities, says the drunk. Why not? the presenter says. So, what's the song? he asks, we're running out of time, my friend. It's a song called 'Stick 'em on the Fire' by Los Van Van.

My father's sudden punch knocks my brother from his chair.

V

The Son

Armando put his arm around my shoulder, hugs me and says sorry. I accepted his apology because he is a man in disgrace and because there are certain moments in this movie – I won't deny it – in which I remember him fondly. You know a man is dying and already his fate leaves you indifferent. You won't save him, you won't deal the death blow, and so you let him go, you let him feel a little better about himself, because what is happening to him now is a process, only in his imagination will anything ever happen to him.

I also want to say something to you all, and to ask you something, my mother says, but I'll wait until María gets here. My sister has just finished her shift at the hotel, probably robbing the place right and left, she's good at that. Only the three of us were home. I had just come back from military service. There was no piñata, no paper hats, no straws, no strawberry cake, no old friends, no uncles, no cousins, no gift-wrapped presents, not even a special dinner waiting for me.

There was my mother, contorted, limp as an old rag, deathly pale. There was my father, staggering, a shadow of himself. There was me, with my army uniform in a cardboard box. There was the telephone and the television. Outside, it was raining, the sky was leaden. It seemed like an afternoon of revelations. My father had apologized. My mother confessed that she had something to say. And so did I. I had gone over and over the speech with which I hoped to free myself from the useless burden I had needlessly taken upon myself.

I've got something to confess: I'm the one who made the phone calls. I'd like to talk about a delicate subject. Listen. I don't know what I was doing, I wasn't myself, life as a soldier is hard. Sometimes, you get bored, you know, there's nothing to do, it started out as a joke, you phone up one day, you say something, you want to stop but you can't, you're having fun, you feel more positive. Please, sit down, I'd like to broach a subject but I'm not sure how to begin. The fake voice, mother, that was me. Remember those strange phone calls? You remember them? They weren't really that important? Good. Well, in any case, it was me, and I'm deeply sorry. You remember them? They were serious? They left you traumatized? Alright, I'm the one responsible. You racked your brain trying to work out who was calling? It was me, no-one else, it wasn't one of your neighbors. I'm not proud of myself, but I did it. I thought about keeping my mouth shut, I thought about saying nothing, but – you know what? – I'm not going to be silent, it just makes me feel like more of a shit than I do anyway. I'm the one who made the phone calls and said all those insulting things. You already knew? I don't have to say anything? What are you asking me? To shut up? Listen, I'll get this over quickly, the phone calls? I made them when I was on sentry duty. There's no easy way to say this, I need you to listen to me and not shout or insult me until I'm finished talking, I need you to listen to what I have to say right to the end. You go mad cooped up in those places, you don't have any friends, you can't trust anyone, there's just an emptiness and an avalanche of time that falls on you with every step.

I couldn't bring myself to speak up. We were sitting in the living room, Armando asking me things and me answering without taking the time to internalize them. My mother had barely reacted when I arrived. On the way home, I had imagined coming through the door and my mother rushing to throw her arms around me, covering me with kisses, shedding a few tears. I had hoped, with a little luck, for the reaction to my homecoming to be as un-sentimental as possible, something that would not make my act of confession more difficult, but now that I had my wish, I found I did not want my mother's lack of emotion, her vacant stare, her reserve. I longed for her warmth, for some little gesture of affection or joy that I was home, however hard it would later be for me to break free.

I asked Armando when he was giving the car back and he said in two days, after my mother's medical check-up. We were going to drive to the hospital in the Nissan. All of us? I asked and he said yes. Have you any objections to coming with us? he asked. No, I said, none, we'll all go to the check-up. I couldn't remember ever having been in a car with Armando, except that day when he got it into his head to drive us to the beach. Your mother wants to go to the hospital on her own, Armando said, we argued about it earlier today. You can't go on your own, I said, and my mother barely blinked. She's gone through the treatment more or less on her own, Armando said, but there's been no improvement.

Perhaps my mother's confession would be significant or dramatic enough to blunt or neutralize the effects of mine, I thought without much hope. Armando did most of the talking, he had already apologized and was rubbing our faces in his affability. I was starting to regret having forgiven him. I should have hung on to my for-giveness and used it as a bargaining chip, a pardon for a pardon.

A little later, María arrived back from work, sopping wet. She kissed us all. She said how happy she was to see me home. She set some parcels on the kitchen table and went to her room to change her clothes. I felt an over-whelming urge to follow her, but decided to hold still. My sister came back into the living room, glanced at us, glanced at my mother, told us to keep an eye on her and started putting the groceries in the fridge.

Now that María's here, I said to my mother, what did you have to tell us? My mother, from the balcony, mumbled something that I don't think anyone heard and then said she had to go to the bathroom and would be right back. Rain was still pattering on the windows and, above this noise, some seconds later, a muffled thud, an unmistakable sound, one that I had never heard, but had only to hear once to know what it was and where it came from.

We all ran to her. Armando and I looked at each other and I was about to let out a hysterical scream when María roughly pushed us aside and elbowed her way through. Go away, she said. María looked at me with contempt. She knew how to deal with this crisis and was happy to brazenly rub my nose in the fact, knowing that I could do nothing, since this was hardly the moment to criticize her arrogance and her bossiness. I'm a better daughter than you are a son, she seemed to say with every helpful gesture. Saying things without saying them is what my sister does best.

Supporting mother's head, she raised her a little so she could breathe more easily. She laid her in the cramped confines of the bathroom. She stretched out her legs and arms to allow the convulsions free rein. A deafening clatter of limbs, as though my mother were a submachine gun. Then, for a moment, she seemed to die.

A gentle, peaceful expression came over her face. A deep groove stitched her lips together. Her cheekbones were jagged, her eyes spent, her eyelids swollen, like pouches filled with dirty water. And yet she wasn't dead. Her left foot twitched continually, moving of its own volition, like the severed tail of a lizard. On her forehead, just above the right eyebrow, there was a trickle of blood.

113

No-one said anything. Only the objects seemed to scream, in dramatic tones. Tiny mouths, inaudible to human ears, opened in the walls and in the mirror. Blood on the rim of the toilet, blood and water in the wash-basin, blood in the gaps between the floor tiles, blood, now black, on her blouse and her glasses. Drops, blotches, pools, violent disproportions. The object imperiously demanded to be cleaned.

I felt ashamed by the fact that I was not the one bleeding. The blood was sticky and gruesome. Its rhythm, slow. There was something reptilian about its pulse. No spurts, no sudden sprays, no gushing arteries. The horror of blood that seems unaware of itself, and still slithers on.

Worse than the sight of the blood was the smell. It made me retch and the retching sent me into a rage. We still could not move my mother from where she lay. Rage made me start cleaning up the blood with a scrubbing brush, and carry on scrubbing even after it was clean, as though I was not simply trying to wash away the dirt, but to rub out the present moment that was already becoming definitive. The wound did not close, the eyelids, the cheekbones, the mouth did not return to their normal state, and still the smell lingered. After a while, I stopped scrubbing.

Armando lifted my mother to her feet and she attempted a few steps, but her drunken legs were shaking. I looked at her beautiful varicose veins, her ankles, shapely in spite of everything, the millimetric moment when her heels made contact with the floor as she attempted to propel herself, to take another step, to project herself forward, as though the heels were the whole person and the rest of the person was nothing more than a dead weight carried on the heels.

Her tongue was tied in knots, a fifty-year-old woman

who was starting to behave like an animal nosing around. She asked nonsensical questions, stammering constantly. Is this what it means to be young again?

She clutched her head and started saying that it hurt. What had happened? We arrived at the clinic and laid her on a metal gurney. Everywhere there were boxes with different stickers, nebulizers, tweezers, gloves, antiseptic creams. My sister reeled off a series of words that I realized I would have to learn: Clobazam, Magnesium valproate, Clonazepam, Lamotrigine.

They put a needle in her vein, sutured the wound. The needle moved through the skin, the thread closed up the gash. There was a swelling on her collarbone, a purple contusion. She had scars in almost every place it is possible to have a scar, and also in places I didn't think possible. My mother as a threadbare shirt that should have been thrown out, like a piece of long outmoded clothing that someone still loves and so continues to mend, patching the holes, re-sewing the buttons, adjusting the collar, taking in the sleeves. Some clothes are like that, comfortable, irreplaceable, clothes you can never bring yourself to get rid of.

She began to regain consciousness and become aware of where she was. My sister and Armando sitting on the edge of the gurney, me standing, pacing up and down. No-one else showed any concern for my mother. The pace of the clinic was not what I'd expected. I realized that a sick person is conspicuous when surrounded by healthy people, but does not stand out among other sick people.

There was a crippled old man with one arm shorter than the other. He took short, stiff steps. His pain was faster than he was. When pain begins to reach us before we reach ourselves, I thought, that's the point when we begin to die. There was a distraught woman begging for some pills. There was a teenager with asthma. There was another woman who burst into the clinic screaming, who seemed to be known to all the staff. I didn't like her. She thought her suffering was greater than everyone else's. She talked about medications and diagnoses as though she were a doctor, but it was obvious that she wasn't.

I went on looking at my mother, her pretty black moccasins with their buckles, like two vinyl hands cupping her feet. I looked at the lines of stitches over her right eyebrow and thought I saw, instead of a suture, one of those blue ties girls used to wear to school back when my mother was a little girl. They told us we could leave, and told us not to miss our appointment at the hospital.

The insufferable woman who had delusions that she was a doctor carried on desperately drawing attention to herself. I took my mother by the shoulders and walked behind, supporting her as she took small, agonizing steps towards the exit, where we summoned a horse and cart to take us home. On the way back, Armando supported my mother. I talked with my sister.

The Mother

It's raining outside and my son is home, though it hardly matters if he's going to leave again. I'll sit still so as not to scare him. It's starting to thunder. I unplug the television, the washing machine and the rest of the appliances. The time has come to confess, as soon as María gets home. I can't carry on with this craziness.

Alright, I have to tell them something: There were no phone calls, no-one ever rang up to insult me, I've only just realized that nothing happened and that it was all a product of my isolation, the ghosts your imagination conjures up and the impossible conversations you find yourself involved in. I'll be brief and direct, no digressions, no bullshit, and none of them will dare question me.

When are you giving back the Nissan? Diego asks Armando. The steel in his voice is much deeper now, gradually he will become an adult and his body and thoughts and physical strength will adjust to this voice, which seems too big for the scrawny boy my son still is. After your mother's check-up, two days from now, Armando says. Are we all going to the hospital in the Nissan? Diego asks. Don't you want to go? Armando says. Yes, of course I want to go, we'll all go to the check-up, Diego says.

It's hardly surprising that he's taken aback, only once has he ever been in one of the cars allocated to his father, for that strange family outing to the beach. Armando did not permit state-owned assets, as he liked to call them, being used for personal reasons. Your mother wants to go to the hospital on her own, he says, we argued about it earlier today. I barely blink, I'll wear them down through exhaustion. She's gone through the treatment more or less on her own, he says, we have let her do it her way, but there's been no improvement.

Anyone who's never been ill thinks that illness is all-encompassing. But if healthy people occasionally fall ill, and occasionally relapse, why do the healthy assume that the sick don't have occasional bursts of health, days when the illness does not manifest itself and our bodies and our minds recover their customary vitality?

They might believe me and they might not. I know what they're thinking, but it was a side-effect of the disease, a delusion brought on by the heavy doses of medication I've been taking. I gradually started to believe it and I felt that everyone else should believe it with me. I've not been deliberately deceiving them for months, it's not like that.

I go out over to the balcony. I stare at the storm clouds, at the rivulets of water streaming down the glass. I endured many downpours during the 'difficult years'. You never knew when they might happen. Sometimes it was no more than a threat, a louring sky. Sometimes they hammered down suddenly, as though angry, and disappeared just as quickly. Sometimes they did not even reach land, but other times, more often, they landed with such force that rainwater formed whirlpools around the storm drains.

I would run into the house with my teacher's briefcase under my arm, shoes wet, tights sodden, blouse plastered to my back, skin covered in goosebumps, bones limp, muscles frozen to the core. My buttocks would stiffen, my nipples stand up. And yet, once home and safe, I felt my features heightened, a certain elegance in an area located between my lips, my nose and my eyes, the focal point of the face, those proportions that affirm or disaffirm beauty.

María arrives home from work soaking wet. She kisses us all and tells Diego she's happy to have him back. She sets some packages on the kitchen table and goes into her bedroom to change her clothes. Then she tells them to keep an eye on me. I feel the need to pee and I head to the bathroom. Are you asleep or awake Mariana? What's going on with you, woman? Why wouldn't someone like me want to die? Why would a person – not just me, anyone – not want to die? Why would a person who is neither dead nor truly alive but has death within reach not want to decide once and for all?

I don't want to die, but not because I want to live. If death is all there is, if death is all that lies ahead, why would I want to rush to meet it, to add death to death? And how is it possible to add death to death, if death is singular and eternal, and whether it comes today, or tomorrow, or twenty years from now makes not the slightest difference since in every case the length of time is the same?

They call my name; I recognize the sounds that make up the name rather than the voice making them. I know what they are saying, but not who they are. The voice is disguised, like the voice in the telephone. It reaches me as though through a funnel.

There is foam in my mouth and blood in my throat. I've never managed to develop a system that alerts me when a seizure is about to happen. They happen and that's that. I should be vigilant, but I keep up my vigilance until the very moment when I am about to black out, conspiring against myself. I want to get up, but I keep postponing the moment, connecting one second to the next and the next, and when that moment passes, which it is, which it has, in the position I find myself in now, in this other moment, that already is, that will be, that has been, crumpled on the floor.

Armando crouches behind me and slips his arms under my shoulders. He lifts me up, I see myself reflected in the bathroom tiles. The building has tilted slightly and is teetering. Within the generalized ache, I feel a throbbing in my collarbone, my forehead, my shoulder and my right knee. Small outposts located in the area bruised during the fall. As consciousness returns, the body emits its signals. The first flash is pain. Suffering is peace.

The Father

People have two separate attention systems, according to experts. Thinking quickly is the first. Strictly speaking, it is almost like not thinking at all – it is acting instantly, instinctively, fluently. The second is thinking slowly, which is overthinking – it involves thinking twice and, if there is time, three times, so that in the end the thinking is focused more on the neurotic loop of the thought process than on the thought itself. I have discovered my problem: I fall into to the second group, and I always wanted to belong to the first.

I rapidly gauged this woman desperately bursting into the clinic and who, from what she was saying, sounded like she was a doctor. I went over to the nurse and discreetly asked the nature of the woman's problem and she told me that the woman had a thirteen-year-old daughter with West Syndrome. I'm sorry, I said, what is West Syndrome? I discovered that the woman's daughter could not move, that she suffered as many as twenty epileptic seizures a day and that right now, when the woman burst into the clinic, she was having difficulty breathing. Is there any cure? I asked. West Syndrome is a degenerative condition, the nurse said, every day she will get a little worse.

I was thinking about this as I left, but not because I wanted to. On the contrary, it was one of those thoughts you want to shake off but cannot, a series of pieces of information that, from the way they interact when brought together, seem to be self-evident. A thirteen-year-old girl, a degenerative illness, more than twenty epileptic fits a day. We were riding in a carriage and I spent the whole journey brooding about this. I was holding Mariana while my children were chatting and the coach driver was screaming insults at the horse to go faster.

Debris gathers above our heads, as though the soft afternoon light was being filtered through a sieve suspended above us. Then this distills, slowly blurring the buildings and the houses in the pueblo, a municipal milk-white film. By now, it had stopped raining. After the showers, everything looked dirtier and grubbier. Spots of mud on my shoes and my pant cuffs.

The carriage sank into every pothole. With every jolt of the wheel, puddles of dirty water exploded and we quivered like springs inside the coach. The rusted iron frame, rather than keeping moving to the trot of the horse, juddered from side to side. The vinyl seats threatened to split at every bump. Steam from the rainstorm rose from the tarmac and mingled with the dust of dried horse manure.

That night was not particularly memorable. I think we ate a few sandwiches, something light. Mariana had said she had something to tell us, but none of us reminded her or asked her anything. She was covered in bruises and those who are ill acquire a moral standing that allows them to act or not to act, to speak or not to speak, while we, the healthy, defer to them after a fashion. We spent a couple of hours sitting in front of the television, although none of us were really paying attention to the programs – we were all engrossed in our own thoughts. I can't say what was distracting the others, but I was still fascinated by the sick thirteen-year-old girl. I found it impossible to imagine such a situation, what exactly it would be like, her illness, her age, the seizures coming minute after minute.

María phoned the neurologist to confirm the appointment and it was then that the neurologist said that he wanted to bring the appointment forward to the following day because he had something important to tell us.

Mariana nodded, whether it was one day or another did not matter to her. Fine by me, Diego said. No problem, I said, we will go tomorrow. Okay, doctor, we'll be at the hospital first thing tomorrow morning, María said.

If we are going in the morning, I think I'll go to bed now and rest up before the drive, I said. Is there gas in the car? María asked. I filled the tank this morning, I said. Make sure you use all the gas before you give it back, Diego said, don't give them anything that belongs to you. I didn't respond, I was too embarrassed. Whatever happens, happens, I thought. I drank a glass of water, emptied my bladder and lay down on the left side of the bed. For the first time in years I wondered whether I too might not be sick. Everyone falling ill, everyone falling to pieces, and me hale and hearty? So began the ordeal.

I don't know whether that night I fell asleep instantly or whether I didn't sleep a wink. Nothing like it had ever happened to me. We know that babies in the womb can cry. It doesn't matter that there is no air, that their lungs are full of amniotic fluid, and that all this means they cannot produce a sound akin to crying. They still cry there, inside, silently, howling and sobbing without anybody knowing.

I couldn't move, couldn't open my eyes. No-one could hear my voice, my cries for help. I was trapped in limbo, a sleep paralysis where the mind is awake and the body still asleep. I wanted to wave but my hands would not move, and this constant immobility was more exhausting than a marathon. What am I missing? I thought. Gas, maybe? Am I a car trying and failing to start, running on empty, sputtering?

Keep a cool head, Armando, I told myself. Concentrate, move slowly, creep out of this limbo, I said to myself. And it seemed to be working. At some point I saw myself sitting up in bed. Everything was in darkness and, lying next to me, in the grip of a seizure, Mariana's entire body was being shaken like a rattle, the brawny arm of her temporal lobe jerking her up and down. I saw myself in slippers, making as little noise as possible, padding into the kitchen, opening the door of the fridge, eyes half-closed, running a hand over my pot belly, feeling the weight of years on my shoulders, a chronic exhaustion, taking out a bottle of water and pouring myself half a glass, the frozen light from the fridge stabbing at my eyes, the sound of my own throat swallowing, the sound of the glass being set down on the counter.

I went back to bed, buried myself under the sheets and only then realized that I had never left, that I had been asleep the whole time, that it was just a dream, though an incredibly vivid dream, with one eye open and one eye closed shall we say. Seen from within, the dream was like a highly realistic painting, by which I mean it wasn't mysterious or intricate or cryptic, it wasn't a dream full of riddles or one that transported me to strange places of forgotten memories of childhood or early infancy. It was a series of innocuous events, the sort of things no-one would dream about.

Who dreams about waking up? Who dreams about getting up and going into the kitchen? Obviously, I was terrified that it might be a delusion, that I was desperate to wake up and my brain was making me believe I was awake. All this I discovered when I got back into bed, because as I did so, I dreamt about getting back into bed, dreaming that I was dreaming, and so it carried on for endless hours, with nothing happening, dreaming that I was asleep, dreaming about a man, about myself, about lying in this same bed where I had been sleeping for who knows how many nights.

The dream was not boring, despite the fact that almost nothing happened except for the involuntary movements of the sleeping bodies of Mariana and me. A shifting torso, a hand gliding from one place to another, the breeze of the fan ruffling the sheets. It was not boring because these were things I had never seen, precisely because I had been asleep. What did I look like when I was asleep? What did my wife look like? And what did my bedroom look like in the early hours, when there was no-one to see?

I thought the night would carry on in this vein until eventually I began to dream about light streaming through the windows, and then about waking up, for real this time, then everyone else waking up and all of us driving to the hospital in the Nissan and later coming home with good news about Mariana, the doctor had said he had noticed a steady improvement in the patient, a positive reduction in focal seizures, and then we carried on with our day, without celebrating but without quarrelling either, me and my son talking the way we used to do, then giving back the Nissan, the keys to the office and all the material comforts that made me a manager, then me accepting the new post assigned to me and spending the rest of my days there, watching the world flash past, understanding everything, not getting involved, not lifting a finger, a mere spectator, just the way it is in dreams.

But no. At some point during the night, the dream divided into a split-screen, on one side I could still see myself sleeping, and on the other, the old nightmare began to play out. In a parking lot, a man standing with his back to me carefully opened the door of a car. A car that, when it roared into life, moved like fear along the black motorway, slowly at first, forty, then eighty and then a hundred and fifty, accelerating to over two hundred. By the side of the road, as always, were the ideological fathers and godfathers. Except that this time I was not traveling in the car, because I was still lying in my bedroom, dreaming that I was asleep.

The car pulled up outside a dark, deserted house in the middle of a field. The driver got out and knocked on the door which was opened by a man. Though nothing was visible, just shades of black on black, I knew from his hat that he was a farmer. They got involved in some sort of transaction and then the farmer closed the door and the driver loaded several sacks and boxes into the trunk of the car. Then we began the long drive back and, just when we had almost reached the parking lot, the dark dream that had been plaguing me for months suddenly changed, and what happened next was brightly illuminated. There came a wail of police sirens and the flash of red and blue lights as a squad car appeared behind the black car, which was not so black, being strobed by lights and sirens, and the black car, that had not once stopped in response to the pleadings of the ideological fathers and stepfathers, meekly pulled over to the curb.

Two officers approached the driver's door; they seemed to be asking to see his documents. The driver did not appear to have them and the officers gestured for him to step out of the car. The driver complied. A few words were exchanged, the officers went around to the trunk, checked the boxes and the sacks. What was in them? What was the driver transporting that – judging from the angry expressions on their faces – so outraged the officers?

They slammed him, spread-eagled, against the car door, frisked, handcuffed and bundled him into the back of the squad car. Then the officers took some of the boxes and sacks and transferred them to the trunk of their own car. While the car that had haunted me through so many nightmares remained parked by the curb, the dream moved away and followed the squad car, its flashing lights piercing the vast darkness for the first time. Some minutes later, the squad car roared in the pueblo, and eventually pulled up outside my building, something that, until that last minute, I had not known would happen. One of the officers climbed the steps and knocked on the apartment door and, realizing they were looking for me, and not wanting to wake anyone, I hurried to answer.

The split-screen dream once more merged into a single image. By now, I didn't know where I was and I didn't care. The officer apologized for waking me at such an ungodly hour. The official formalities completed, he informed me that he had arrested one René González in a '95 Nissan belonging to the State, that the individual in question claimed that it was my car, that he was my driver and was acting on my orders.

Why did they arrest you? I said. I don't know, you tell me, the driver said, standing in the doorway of my home, but acting as though it were his. At any other point in my life I would have known what to say, but right then I didn't. Is he or is he not your driver? the officer asked, his face suddenly that of the devil. In that instant, everything changed.

The Daughter

The trip to the hospital takes three and a half hours. We walk along the road, my mother and I, hitching a lift. Mamá seems a little happier, despite everything that has happened. My father has ended up at the police station, and my brother has gone to find out why.

We catch a bus and then a lieutenant colonel's jeep drops us off outside the hospital. We arrive at the neurologist's office fifteen minutes before our appointment. My mother has a lunatic smile that won't go away. One of the other patients takes out a flask and offers us some coffee, saying she's been there all night. I thank her for the gesture, but I don't want to talk to anyone. If I accept the coffee, I'll be walking into a trap. She'll start prattling on and we'll be forced to respond.

At precisely 8.30 a.m. the neurologist ushers us in. He doesn't care that there were others in front of us. We walk along a dirty, dimly lit corridor and go into the third office on the right. Opposite, there is an admissions ward. Almost all of the beds are empty, made up with lime green sheets. I can hear the grumbling of patients but I can't see any. We sit on metal chairs, look around the consulting room. There is dust everywhere, papers and yellow forms are piled on shelves eaten away by termites. The venetian blinds are broken, the smell of the place is unpleasant. A smell of ampoules and injections, of contaminated syringes and bloody cotton swabs.

This is not a neurologist's office, I think. The walls are hung with posters about preventing breast cancer and the terrible damage cigarettes inflict on the airways and the lungs. The cancer cell is the only cell that is immortal. When there is nothing left for it to devour, it devours itself, but nothing can kill it.

The doctor who ushered us in reappears with another man. They both introduce themselves. Next to the neurologist is a specialist oncologist. This must be his office. They say they have noticed a number of irregular markers, that this is why they asked to speak to a family member. I am here, but they have still not acknowledged me. They speak to my mother; she does not answer. And you are...? one of them says. I'm the daughter. Ah, the daughter! Perfect, he says.

The medical logorrhea goes on for some time, but my brain pinpoints and files away the important points. They are going to begin a new trial, they say. They are going to order new magnetic resonance images, new encephalograms and new CT scans. They are not convinced that the temporal lobe epilepsy is the result of the chemotherapy prescribed for my mother after her radical hysterectomy. And there is more. They have reviewed the case from the beginning. They are struck by the fact that they have not yet come up with a definitive answer. They have spent months groping about for an answer, prescribing medications whose effectiveness has been proven in other patients. My mother's expression seems both to advance and retreat.

There is something they need to know. The neurologist asks her whether she has actually followed the course of treatment. Have you been taking the tablets, Mariana? My mother does not answer. Her hands twitch. Dark circles bloom under her eyes. I slump back in the metal chair. The day before, in the coach on the way home, my brother and I were talking about things whose appearance can be deceptive, like the yellow chickens that, during the 'difficult years', families in the pueblo force-bred in wire cages under incandescent lights so hot that in the end they all died. They seem noble, he said to me, but chickens are cannibals.

I ask them why they have doubts. Not all patients react in the same way, every body is unique. The results of Mariana's biopsy indicated only a small, insignificant tumor, the oncologist explains. After the operation, her mother was not recommended such an aggressive course of cytotoxic drugs. The oncologist wants to know how Mariana got the prescription for the course of chemotherapy. Who authorized it? Why did she deliberately poison herself? Mariana does not open her mouth.

Toe pecking occurs in early clutches, especially when, for some reason, newly hatched chicks are not fed within the first forty-eight hours. Before they can think, the more dominant chicks have learned to peck the toes of the weaker chicks.

I don't know, doctor, she says after a moment, the smile never leaving her face. I just couldn't carry on, she says. Carry on with what? A minute or two passes in which no-one says anything. I kiss the top of her head. She has ceased to be my mother. We will stay together, in silence, to the end, but she has ceased to be my mother. I cannot be upset by something done by someone who no longer has anything to do with me.

Pecking happens during molting, it can be triggered by the little drops of blood left when feathers are pulled out. Vent pecking is triggered by the reddish color of the cloaca, when laying is about to start. Then there's the savage pecking in growing chicks. Feathering begins at about three weeks. The chicks peck at each other's backs, at the root of the tail, sometimes they even end up pecking the intestines.

All the love she has managed to store up in me would be enough, would never run out, but between us there would no longer be a daily love, one renewed each day.

According to my brother, to withstand a night on sentry duty, a soldier on military service needs two things. The first is to make sure you have a raw recruit with you for as much time as possible. You quickly discover that, in these conditions, company, in any form, is a good thing. And it is not the duty sentry who needs to be kept entertained, but his companion, so that he does not leave. The second is to master the art of head-nodding, which is not a deep sleep, or even a doze, but a larval state that any half-decent soldier with more than six months' experience should be able to achieve.

I thank the doctors and promise them I'll oversee the treatment. The doctors say they'll visit, that they don't want to pressure us with questions right now. We say our goodbyes. It takes us another three hours to get home. On the way back I hug her and run my fingers through her hair; she sobs. When we get back, we take a deep breath. My mother sings the song about the old stewing hen and starts to dance.

There are various causes that can trigger cannibalism in poultry. Excessive heat, overcrowding in the hatchery, especially around the feeders and the drinking troughs, poor diet and a lack of protein. Weak or crippled chicks suffer a lot. In battery cages, boredom is an inherited vice. And it is this boredom that is the main reason why innocuous chickens, terribly innocuous chickens, lethally innocuous chickens, end up pecking at each other, eating each other's entrails.